INTRODUCTION

In the early days of 1910, when Glacier National Park was established, United States Army soldiers were the acting rangers for the park service. These were the men that patrolled the park borders and backcountry. In those early years, there were legal homesteads within the park that were used as hunting and trapping cabins. These homesteads are still privately owned within the park today. Once the park was officially vested, park policy no longer permitted hunting or trapping within the preserve. These activities needed to be enforced. The Park Service was soon established within the Department of the Interior. At that time, Park Service rangers replaced the Army soldiers. Ranger stations and patrol cabins were built along the park's perimeter, with a few of them built in the interior. One such backcountry ranger station was Belly River. This valley was a mecca for large game and furbearers. That created a problem for the newly hired rangers. Few knew anything about trapping for furs, and the hunting of elk, deer and bear. The rangers were ineffective at enforcing game violations. When Park Service management realized this, the superintendent determined that in order to catch hunters and trappers, they needed to hire hunters and trappers. A short time later, he proclaimed, "To catch a poacher, you need to hire a poacher."

Joe Cosley, a half-Indian Caucasian, was hired as a ranger to keep poachers out of Belly River. The book, "Belly River's Famous Joe Cosley" is written about him, and is worth reading, if one is interested in the men of Glacier Park. Joe was an excellent trapper himself and had trapped and poached throughout his life. Once Joe was hired, he kept the valley free of poachers. Being an excellent trapper himself, he couldn't resist trapping the plentiful beavers, muskrats, pine martens (sable), long- and short-tailed weasels and mink, in the area. Back in the early part of the century, it was reported that he had trapped $10,000 worth of furs in one year, out of the Belly River Valley alone, from the same area that he was supposed to be protecting. Joe had the best of tack for his horse, and was also known for being a very fancy dresser, having boots with spurs inlaid into the heels. These were expenses a normal ranger could not afford on a government paycheck. He was also blessed with a charismatic personality. Everyone liked Joe Cosley. Eventually, he had trouble with the Park Service and was relieved of his duties, but he continued sneaking into Belly River to trap. He was finally apprehended and placed in jail in Belton, Montana, just outside of West Glacier. Likable Joe was freed by a friend and escaped back to Belly River, to pick up a cache of pelts he had stashed and wanted to sell. His jail escape and hike from Belton to Belly River was a monumental marathon. Joe accomplished this hike in midwinter. That should have been entirely impossible. He hiked through deep snow, climbed over snow-covered passes and accomplished it all in one day. Joe eventually faded into history as he aged, and his poaching days expired.

Since Joe's time, there have been no serious, recorded poaching incidents perpetrated in the Belly River Valley. However, there is a rumor that one permanent ranger, back in the days when rangers stayed in the valley all winter, was involved in such an operation. The story goes like this. A Canadian farmer, and this particular ranger, had an agreement to ignore each other's misdeeds. In the fall, the Canadian farmer would cross the border into the valley and shoot an elk, while the Belly River Ranger would hitch up his horse and

RANGER ON THE RUN

ERNEST LOMMATSCH III

wagon, drive across the border to the farmer's land, and kill a cow for his winter meat. This was their mutual agreement. Most say it's a rumor; I believe differently.

The story you are about to read is fiction, with many park facts intertwined. Any resemblance to real persons in this tale is purely accidental, coincidental, and unfounded.

I hope that this book will enlighten you with an education about many park elements that are factual. The fictitious parts are what they are. This story was written entirely for your education and entertainment.

1

It was the fall of 1979. It was the darkest part of the morning, an hour before the sun rose above Gable Mountain. The frost crunched beneath the horses' and my feet as I packed my gear and saddled up to leave the backcountry for the season. It was late fall and I knew the snow would fall again soon, but at this time of year it would stick and blanket the ground until spring. Recently, there had been a terrible storm that took out communications in the park, or at least to this backcountry station. I dreaded leaving this remote valley in Glacier National Park, but I wasn't prepared with enough supplies, to stay as a volunteer through the winter months. Besides, when the snows finally did fall, the road, six-and-a-half miles away, would not be plowed for the winter, and leaving this area would be a tough, two-day trek to St. Mary Ranger Station on foot. As a seasonal ranger, I had officially been terminated from duty a few weeks before and was currently on volunteer status since the end of September. I had requested a year's leave of absence from my teaching job at a high school just south of the park in a small logging town. I decided a year ago I'd like to stay as late into the fall as possible at this secluded backcountry station and leave before becoming snowed in for the long winter. Park officials were expecting me sometime before the 15th of November, but due to the oncoming winter and a few widespread snow flurries, I decided to leave my post two weeks early.

It takes an entire day to get the stock packed up to head out to the trailhead at the road, remove the pack saddle, my saddle, load the stock in the truck, and drive to St. Mary District Ranger Station. When arriving at St. Mary ranger station, I'd have to unload the stock truck and dismantle the packs, put away the tack in the barn, and then officially check out from my last month's volunteer employment. I was actually getting an early start this morning, having mantied-up all the gear yesterday and balancing the loads for the packsaddles. It was still taking me well over an hour to make ready for the journey out.

Finishing the loads on the Decker packsaddles and hitching them down, I entertained one last look around the station and outbuildings to make sure all was secure for the cruel winter ahead. The shutters were on, and the bear boards beneath the windows were in place. In past years the grizzlies and black bears had managed to enter inside the station in search of food, creating substantial damage in their search. Besides, grizzlies never travel out the same way they come in, adding to the clean up and restoration of the old station. All appeared to be in place for the winter. It was time to depart with the loaded-up stock and ride out to the trailhead. I detested leaving this home-away-from-home for another six months. This is God's country, smack dab in the middle of Big Sky country and within the borders of the magnificently beautiful Glacier National Park. I began reminiscing about the last six months of solitude and the daily scenery that was at an end for me this season. It was time to head back to civilization, with electricity, hot-and-cold running water, telephones, traffic and a multitude of people.

The sun peeked out over the top of Gable Mountain, shining its morning, tangerine alpenglow across the Belly River Valley, boasting of the awesomeness of the high peaks around me, and giving me the feeling that I was looking from the bottom of the Grand Canyon. These peaks stretched up from the valley floor, poking the sky with their 10,000-foot elevation. They appeared closer than the three miles from my residence, here at the ranger station. The majesty of the mountains surrounding Belly River Ranger Station is a never-ending display. The magic of the mountains gives them different personalities as the sun navigates across the sky, casting shafts of shadows across the steep, eroded, earth toned cliff faces.

The two-hour ride out to the trailhead and customs highway offers a very pleasurable, panoramic journey through the low flatlands of the valley floor, as one travels through long, wide meadows, with mountains rising abruptly on the meadows' edges. The meadows companion up with the slow-moving river that meanders lazily through and around them. This is unique habitat for the abundance of wildlife that makes this their home. It's a perfect niche where beaver, muskrat, pine martin (sable), mink, badger, Columbian ground squirrels, rodents, deer and a few small- to medium-sized elk herds make their home range. In bygone years, when the park was established in 1910, and into the early 1940s, poaching did occur here. Poaching of elk and deer, along with trapping beaver, martin and mink, was a mainstay for these huntsmen. The abundance of native prairie meadow grasses is perfect elk browse. Hunters within the park's borders do not disturb these ungulates in their open range solitude. Elk herds flourish here with bulls growing massive bodies, with antlers commonly spreading out to seven or eight points on each side. This habitat creates huge antlers, with head capes worth hundreds, if not thousands of dollars each to a buyer for mounting. That doesn't account for the price of the fabulously lean, tasty elk meat, which could render up to two hundred butchered pounds per animal.

A chilly, faint breeze nipped at my bare skin in the morning chill; cobalt skies promised a clear sunny day ahead. The solitude of the morning was abruptly disturbed by the crack of rifle fire in the near distance ahead of me. Again, another shot from the same direction. The mountains echoed the sound, making it difficult to pinpoint the exact origin of the reports, but I knew the general vicinity of where the shots had originated.

I quickly dismounted and led the stock off the trail to tie them to some trees in the small poplar grove I was traveling through. The pack animals were only semi-hidden from sight near the trail. I grabbed my daypack that contained my pistol, flex-cuffs, ammo, citations, first aid kit, camera, compact binoculars, canteen, a little food and some other useful paraphernalia. I mounted back up on my horse, leaving the pack animals, and proceeded in a roundabout direction toward where the shot had been fired. My route was in a transitional fringe at the edge of the meadow, just within the tree line, where my movement would not be easily or quickly detected. Elk were moving in all directions from the meadow into the shelter of the woods. As soon as they observed or smelt my presence, they bolted away. I was approaching where the rifle had been fired, because I could hear faint voices in the distance. I dismounted and tethered my horse in a thicket of quaking aspen between two small meadows, to begin my approach on foot, staying within the cover of trees. I crept cautiously toward the voices, knowing that poachers in a federal reserve like a national park are subject to federal prosecution, imprisonment, huge dollar fines and confiscation of firearms, horses, tack, and transport vehicles used in the unlawful activity. The men involved in this type of illegal activity were well aware of the consequences and would likely try anything to get away scot-free, even if that meant murder. I needed to identify these people, and then make my departure without being noticed. Many thoughts raced through my mind as I snuck through the brush and trees toward the voices. Whoever these folks were must have figured that, as in years past, the ranger had left the valley weeks before. Once the ranger had left for the season, they had a free ticket to do their personal trophy hunting for fun and profit. I wondered if this was the case, and how long this activity had been going on.

The voices became louder as I closed in, and I could only make out a few words. There was still a small poplar grove to creep through before I could possibly get a visual on them. My face stung at the same instant that I heard the report of a rifle. The poplar tree just inches from my right cheek exploded spraying bark, moisture, and wood fibers above my right eye and along my cheek. Momentarily stunned and surprised, I immediately dropped to the ground as I faintly heard what sounded like the rifleman jacking another shell into the chamber for a followup shot. I scrambled forward; staying low. Then I quickly stood up and began a sprint into a thicket of lodgepole pines a few yards to my right. Another shot rang out and I heard the bulled whiz over my shoulder and slam against a tree behind me. I then cut to my right at a dead run, knowing a target moving laterally through the trees would be harder to hit than one running directly away. The trees also created obstacles for the shooter, keeping him from a clear, unobstructed shot with the broken-up cover. Again, another shot. However, the bullet never made it close to me far as I could tell. The trees and my movement were making it impossible for the pursuer to get a clear shot. I dropped down on a knee and looked back when I felt I was clear from fire. I saw the shooter who was less than 200 yards behind me, mounting his horse. There was no possible way he would be able to ride through the density of the woods I was now in. He would have to pursue me on foot. I must have been less than 100 yards from him when the first shot was fired. The rider had a dark complexion, either from the sun or his being of a different nationality. The eastern border of the park lies against a Native American Reservation. That reservation was within 10 miles of me, and the Canadian border was five and a half miles to the north, where another reservation lay beyond. I watched the rider turn and ride in the direction of the voices.

I removed my daypack and grabbed my stainless, Smith & Wesson .44 Magnum revolver and strapped it on my hip. I had six shells in the revolver and six more that I transferred to my pocket for quicker reloading. I wished I had taken the bulky hand radio from my saddlebags, in the hope that the radio repeaters on the mountain were working again after last week's storm. My horse was at least a quarter mile to the south of me. I couldn't return to my horse, as they would soon discover the animals and ambush me if I tried. These guys would soon figure out they needed to find me, terminate me and get rid of my remains in order to flee this escapade. I also knew the park personal would not be expecting me today, but in two weeks, to sign out for the season. If I didn't show up then, they would come looking for me on foot, horseback, snowshoes or x-country skis, depending on the weather. I figured the case would likely be closed after an intensive search with no results. The cause of death, they would surmise, would be a fatality from an accident of some type, like a grizzly attack, a fall during a climb, a river ford drowning or any number of different scenarios. I had to escape this and stay alive to tell about it.

My only hope was to get out to the nearest road, but I knew they would soon move someone quickly to wait in ambush for me there. The other alternative was to head back toward the headwaters of the Belly River. On the other hand, I could take the trail by Elizabeth Lake over Red Gap Pass, or the Ptarmigan Tunnel Trail to Many Glacier. I could also possibly climb to the southeast over Ahern Pass or over the divide, to the U.S. end of Waterton Lake. I had many options to choose from. All of these possibilities would take time and effort, adding up to many miles of foot travel. I would often have to dodge the men who would be hunting me during my escape. Going back to the horse was out of the question. I also needed to obtain a better description of these felons, and how many of them there were. That thought was something I was not considering very strongly, as I could be killed in the process. At the moment, they had no idea where I was. I also had no clue as to how many of them there were, or where they might be scattered throughout in the valley.

2

I headed west and crossed the Belly River on an old logjam, then doubled back, upstream from the area of the gunshots and voices. Dodging quickly in the cover, I figured no one was yet following me yet. I continually checked my back trail. I climbed up a hillside across the river from where the barely-audible voices were coming from. Taking out my binoculars, I searched the area. I spotted them about a quarter mile from me. I counted six men including the one that shot at me, and he was pointing in the direction where he had last seen me. Two gutted elk were lying nearby, a few yards away. Both elk were trophies, worth good money on the black market. I made note of the color of their horses. Farther beyond these men were half a dozen pack animals with Decker packsaddles. Each man had darkish hair and appeared to be of American Indian descent. Another mounted rider rode in at a gallop from behind them. That made seven, and I hoped there were no more.

I watched them closely for a few minutes, as they were drawing in the dirt what looked like some sort of a search plan. I attempted to get a hint of what they were up to from their hand gestures, but to no avail. Hearing another shot off in the distance, I knew there were more men than what I was seeing through the binoculars. The group looked up and one of the individuals mounted his horse and rode toward the shot.

My odds of survival were becoming less with each additional hunter. How many were there, actually? I watched, hoping to get some sort of design of their plan. Another rider came to the gathering, leading my horse and both pack animals. I was conjuring up negative imaginings that I might be doomed, as more and more men kept appearing. I had to think and act fast if I wanted to see the sun rise again. If I were to die, I was determined to take as many with me as I could, even if I only had a pistol and 12 shots. I wished I had a rifle. With a pistol, each shot would have to count, and I would need to be in relatively close range. They had rifles. I would have to outfox them, and shoot them one at a time at close range, in some sort of surprise ambush.

Those guys knew I was still in the vicinity, and on foot. I had to either go north or south from there. The last shot came from the north, and I figured there were more men in that direction than there was south, closer to the ranger station. There would be an all-out manhunt once the word got out that there was a ranger on the loose that had discovered their activity. I decided to take a long way out which could be a couple of different routes. I was willing to take the gamble because I knew the terrain and territory better than they. I lived here and hiked all around the area for the last three summer seasons. That was my greatest advantage. I considered that the best possibility would be to work myself away from them carefully, without running smack dab into any of them. I decided that heading southward toward the Mokowanis Junction Trail and up to Stony Indian Pass was my best possibility. My pace was cautious, as I kept an eye out for any movement ahead or behind. My gray ranger uniform shirt and forest green pants were like camouflage that blended well into the woods around me. I wished the broad leaves were still clinging to the broadleaf plants, as the extra cover would have been helpful. However, the leaves had dropped over a month ago.

I began side hilling toward the south a little ways above the valley floor, where I might have a clearer view below, to detect any movement. I kept my traverse cautious; trying to gain as much ground away from the majority of them, as possible. Above me were talus slopes beyond the trees I was using for cover. If I were to get on those rocky slopes above, I'd be spotted quickly. I hiked for 20 more minutes then stopped to glass the area below to see if I could find my manhunters. Maybe I could figure what their search plan looked like. I finally viewed eight horsemen about a mile behind me to the north. They were spread out, riding upriver on the valley floor in my direction. There were four on each side of the river, spaced about a hundred yards apart, while staying parallel to each other, combing the area. They all held rifles across their saddles as they rode. I was at least a mile ahead of them and higher than the end rider, on my hillside.

I climbed farther uphill toward the talus slope's edge, staying in tree cover. Years of slides and runoff had created rubbles of rocks that formed small, shallow, cave-like openings a few feet deep, into the mountain. There would be a good vantage point, as I could see clearly past the trees, being barely above the tree line. If I were seen and pinned on those rocks, the bullet ricochets could cut me to ribbons. I would not be staying here long. A creek bed with a small trickle of water ran nearby and I was thirsty. I hunkered down in front of the dark backdrop of a cave to glass the area over and over, looking for movement below. I had worked up a good sweat. The sun had been up for two hours and it appeared a clear autumn day was developing. I shed my down vest and medium-weight jacket, stuffing them into my pack. I checked for the rations I had in my pack: two cans of tuna, two peanutbutter bars, one dry Gatorade drink mix, a pack of gum, three cups of coffee crystals, plus two hot-chocolate mix packs along with my Sierra cup. This was all the food I was carrying. My first aid kit held my matches, wax paper for starting fires, a few assorted bandages, gauze pads and a roll of adhesive tape. The kit, being plastic, was basically waterproof, and kept the matches dry, even in wet weather. As an extra precaution from dampness, I kept my stick matches inside an empty 12-gauge shotgun shell with a 20-

gauge shell slipped over the matches that fit snugly inside the 12-gauge shell. I would need matches once night came and the temperatures dropped into the freezing zone and below. Then I'd need the warmth of a fire but would need to build one in a place where it would not be detected. Without a fire, I would get hypothermia and be yielded unconscious or dead by morning.

I continued up the ravine through cover of the alders, into some rock rubble. I took off my pack and sat down and watched for my pursuers, feeling I was safely hidden in the rocks and the alder shadows behind me. Within a few moments, I located them. With my binocs, I could still make out eight riders, four on each side of the river, en route up the valley where I was heading. Their progress was slow and methodical. If I had been in their searching area, I'd have most likely been spotted, as there is little cover to hunker down and hide in on the valley floor. The lodgepole pine they rode through had very few lower branches for any kind of hiding cover, and brush was sparse there.

I glassed the valley again. It soon revealed one more individual on his horse guarding the meadow trail north, toward the highway. There was probably someone else stationed at the road itself. The roadway was gated at the Canadian border customs this time of year, creating a dead end. There would be no entry into Canada until next spring, when the customs station reopened for the season. The Park Service no longer patrolled this section of road, as there would be no traffic using it this late into the fall. My stock truck was parked at the U.S. Customs station, behind their buildings, on the U.S. side of the gate. The predators' trucks could possibly be at the trailhead near the Customs entry. They might have ridden in from the reservation border on the park's eastern boundary. That would make their entry an overnight camping trip, somewhere in the thick woods of Lee Ridge, before entering the valley.

I was still contemplating my situation with an eye toward my best alternative for escape. I could head south to Stoney Indian Pass or branch off and travel cross-country, to hike over Chaney Glacier and climb over the notch above it. No trail existed there but I had hiked this route in the past as a shortcut to Fifty Mountain Campsite. It was not a dangerous hike or climb. From either saddle, I could drop down to the Highline Trail and hike to the Going-to-the-Sun Road near the loop or hike back north toward Goat Haunt Ranger Station, along the Valentine Creek Trail. From there, the Going-to-the-Sun Road would be a long, thirty-five-mile-plus trek, which includes a five thousand foot elevation gain, to pass over either of those two divides. It appeared these were my only options to vanish from this posse.

3

I grabbed my pack and pulled out my canteen. I drank my fill, and then refilled the canteen in the small creek nearby. With the pack back on, I began walking through the alder and poplar into the coniferous woods, traveling in a southerly direction. I carefully did my best to stay out of sight from below, and to move slowly enough so as not to attract attention in sparsely covered places.

I had walked almost a mile, and checked my watch to confirm my distance. I wondered if the searching riders had come across the rocky rubble site I had been in. I might have left a fresh footprint in the mud by the creek where I filled the canteen. In the future, I'd need to be more careful by checking my immediate back trail, to see that I had not left any sign of my existence with a boot print.

I turned downward off the side of the hill toward an old, unmaintained fire trail. Traveling on that trail would be faster than the woods and brushy hillside I was hiking through. I was sure these vigilantes were unaware of this old trail. They had no reason to come this far up the valley, as the big game didn't hang out here. There was hardly any grass growing under the lodgepole and spruce trees in this acidic soil, so grazing animals stuck to the rich, grassy, open meadows of the valley floor to the north. This area grew low shrubs, such as spiria, helborne, thimbleberry, cinquefoil, elderberry, wild currant, bear grass and meadow rue, with a few scattered huckleberry bushes sprinkled in. I was betting on them not having knowledge of this old trail. They would be searching through these grounds soon. My progress was much faster on this trail. I was hiking about three miles an hour toward the upper valley on my way to the passes. A few blow-downs slowed my pace, but I was still moving ahead at a satisfying clip. My long legs were able to step over the majority of the blow-downs that most persons would have to slowly climb over. I had a good feeling about making it up to the valley headwall within three hours. I was breaking a good sweat, and was hoping the poachers were still moving in their slow, methodical pursuit.

I had been hiking for an hour, and veered upward on the side hill to get a look down into the valley. Searching with my field glasses, I could see only one of the horsemen near the river, still riding in my direction. I couldn't see the rest of them. I was not elevated high enough, and the dense evergreens blocked most of my view. Eventually, I saw one more horseman on the far side of the hill and knew there were still eight in the group; they had not split up. It was close to lunchtime for me, as I hadn't eaten since four o'clock in the morning, and that was seven hours before. I grabbed a peanutbutter bar from my pack and inhaled it, then washed it down with water from my canteen. I was still hungry, but I needed to conserve the food I had left. I had a long trip on foot ahead of me and would need more caloric intake later, to gain my freedom from this lynching posse.

Replacing my pack, I continued up the valley. My shirt was soaked with sweat. At the next creek, I filled my canteen and continued on. In the back of my mind, I was glad that during my past three summers, I had explored off the trails as much as I had. I had become intimately familiar with this backcountry topography. I had bushwhacked off the trails to climb peaks, walk through alpine meadows and hanging gardens, and went to places just because they were there. This was my backyard, and my familiarity with these grounds would be my ace in the hole. My mind raced through many thoughts about both passes and how I might stay concealed. Both passes were above the tree line and I would be walking through vast, open alpine meadows. In most cases, I was taller than the subalpine fir that survived there. At that altitude, the winter snow shortened the growing season due to the extreme depth of it, and to the drifts that lay there late into summer. These subalpine trees sprouted in spread-out clusters, with lots of open ground between the clumps. If by chance a gunman had been posted in that area, I would be seen, stalked and terminated rather quickly. I needed to be extremely alert and quick if I was to traverse any of these alpine areas. At either pass, I wouldn't be safe from rifle fire, because of the lack of cover. My negative imaginings and logic were bouncing around in my head again. If someone was there already, my effort would have been for nothing, and I would likely meet my demise.

I was approaching the junction where the two valleys converged. I decided to take the southwest route over Chaney Glacier through the notch above. Sneaking slowly, I worked my way up the valley floor. I knew that if a rifleman was placed at the junction, on a rocky outcropping above this trail, he could easily see the confluence of the junction and I'd be a very easily seen target. I kept my eyes open to any slight movement while staying off the maintained trail, in the shelter of the undergrowth. As I snuck down toward the trail, in cover, there were shod horses tracks heading in the same direction I was headed. Were they heading up to Stoney Indian Pass? If so, there were more men than I had seen. Two sets of tracks were traveling this way.

For how many autumns had these daredevils entered this balanced ecosystem and victimized the elk, and who knows what else? If they successfully killed me and destroyed my remains, they could continue hunting the valley for a few more years, although the next time they would be more cautious, calculating and vigilant before entering here. They were well organized for this escapade, probably making decent money on the black market for trying some-thing so bold and daring. Else they liked the challenge, the excitement, or being on a hunt with longtime friends. They were all in panic mode because of my unexpected presence. They had surprised a ranger who was still in the area, and who had witnessed the felony they committed.

I stepped forward quietly, taking care not to move too quickly or create noise in the brush. I arrived at the junction by staying off the trail and easing myself in the direction of Chaney Glacier. The air was still and crisp in the autumn noon. I froze instantly when I heard a horse blow and stomp. The sound came from in front of me beyond a clump of subalpine fir and spruce trees. I moved closer to see if my enemy was tending to the animal. Closing the distance in the direction of the sound, I saw the rump of a sorrel through a small opening in the branches. Taking one slow step after another, I closed in on the horse as quietly as a church mouse. When the sorrel was in full view, I saw a dapple-gray horse tethered on the opposite side of the sorrel. Both horses were saddled to ride. Slowly, I closed the span to improve my view of the situation and the grounds surrounding the stock. That was when I saw a rifle in the scabbard on the near sorrel horse. I stopped and waited, watching for anybody or any movements near the horses. I saw no one. With my pistol in hand, cocked and ready, I needed to retrieve that rifle for my survival. It was imperative for my survival. It would give me the distant killing power and accuracy that a pistol could never provide.

Looking and listening for the slightest sound or movement, I wormed forward toward the sorrel. As I approached it, I noticed that the other saddle's rifle scabbard was empty. All of a sudden, the horses were alert to my presence, as their ears turned toward me, and their heads quickly followed, to stare. That concerned me, as an onlooker would know something was amiss. I froze immediately, pistol ready. All was quiet. It seemed that no one was around. I crept slowly toward the sorrel. I reached out my left hand and began touching him gently.

"Easy now," I said, whispering to the horse softly. "Easy," I said as I touched the horse's rump.

Stepping forward, I reached up and slid the rifle out of the scabbard from beneath the fender of the stirrup. I un-cocked my pistol and returned it to its holster. My hopes were high as I finally felt I had a chance of staying alive by possessing a rifle. It was a lever-action Winchester 45-70 caliber with open sights. I cracked open the action slightly, to see if the chamber had a round in it. It did. Satisfied it was loaded and ready to fire, I closed the action.

Both horses perked up their ears and turned their heads, facing the same direction. Was someone coming? I instantly dropped to one knee facing where the horses were staring. I could hear what sounded like footsteps coming through the brush of a narrow game trail, no more than 50 feet away. I surprised him, as he looked upward toward the horses and saw me. He flinched in surprise and began to lift his rifle but I had already aimed and had a bead on him. I had to shoot or be shot. I squeezed the trigger and the rifle bucked, sounding its booming report as the bullet struck him between his tan jacket lapels, leaving a small dime size crimson hole in the shirt, on his chest. He back stepped when the slug struck him, and began to raise his rifle to aim his rifle to shoot. My rifle bucked again, the shot jerking his shoulder as he fired.

The sorrel behind me dropped to the ground. The shot was over my head and struck the horse. The animal fell to the ground and heaved a heavy last breath, while his hindquarters twitched a last couple of kicks. The bullet had struck him right in the neck bone. His vertebra had been instantly shattered and his life was drained from him. I levered my rifle ready to fire, then slowly walked over to the dead man. He appeared to be of Native American descent, but I wasn't positive. I knew him by sight only. He lived around the Saint Mary area on the park's eastern border. He owned an eatery and beer bar just outside of town. He was dead. I quickly turned back to the horses and checked the saddlebags for more shells, and whatever else might be helpful to me in my situation. I found a box of bullets with ten shells left inside, and reloaded the carbine.

I needed to get the heck out of there quickly, while paying atten-tion around me. I emptied the saddlebags on the ground and found an apple and a sandwich that I stuffed into my pack. I knew the other horse had a rider that must have heard the shots and would be returning to see what the shooting was about. The mountains had echoed the rifles' reports. Soon, others would be coming to where the shots were fired. I cut the cinch strap of the dead horse's saddle, long enough to create a makeshift sling for the rifle. Later, I might need both hands free for climbing. My two options of going over the passes were currently spoiled by the noise of the gunfire. Someone would likely suspect I'd be heading over one of the two passes to escape, and exit the valley. If I didn't leave there quickly, I could be boxed in at the head of the valley. I needed to do the unexpected and head back down the valley from where I had come, traveling toward the posse search party.

I cut the other horse's cinch, making it difficult to saddle again. It would take time to re-cinch the saddle and tend to the dead body. I also cut the saddle cinch short on the dead horse's saddle. That would give me more time to flee.

As I turned to leave, a tug jerked my left shoulder. At the same moment, I heard a rifle report. I quickly grabbed my pack and rifle, and ran laterally into some thick cover. No more shots were fired. I turned to look around and saw a man carrying a rifle, walking down the slope on the far side of the horses. He looked to be about 100 yards away. He had a scope rifle. "Damn," I was thinking, "that's not good for my situation, with that kind of long distance accuracy."

I felt the warm wetness of blood trickling down the back of my left shoulder. I was fortunate. I think it had just clipped the top of my shoulder. It was a grazing shot and only tore through the muscle on top of my shoulder, near my neck. I was lucky it wasn't my head, or pierced lower into my chest or shoulder, and broke bone. I was still able to move my arm freely. I must have been moving when the bullet struck me. He shot from a fair distance, and it was likely an off-hand shot, without a forearm rest to steady his rifle. I could have been injured a whole lot worse, but I suspect he made a quick, impulsive shot.

I sprinted down the valley a short ways into some deep cover and stopped. In my back trail, I could hear swearing, and I realized my shootist had seen his dead friend, dead horse, and the saddles with cut cinches. I was sure he would not try to follow me. He wouldn't come after me then, knowing I was armed with a rifle. Besides, he would have to travel on foot, off trail, and he was alone.

4

A new escape plan came to mind. I needed to meander through some thick timber and brush, up the steep mountainside, and then climb a talus slope where a horse would be unable to travel. I had to get to White Crow Basin, north of the base of Mt. Cleveland. My destination was to go back down the valley about four miles from where I was. I would need to climb the ridge that came off Mt. Cleveland and joined Kaina Mountain. Both mountains are in excess of nine thousand five hundred feet. Mt. Cleveland is the tallest mountain in the Park, and is just over 10,000 feet in height. The narrow, rocky and steep ridge of cliffs that joins the two mountains together appears like the teeth of a ripsaw facing upward on its jagged, elongated, stretched-out saddle. This ridge is almost eight thousand feet high. Climbing over this summit would drop me down near Goat Haunt Ranger Station, at the head of Waterton Lake. Once there, I could start the generator and radio for help. I hoped that the radio repeater in that area was still working. The ranger station also had winter rations laid away for the February snow depth course. This ranger station also contained warm sleeping bags and a bunk.

There were no trails where I was traveling, and I was gambling that I could find a route. I had never spent a lot of time in the basin and I wasn't very intimate with the topography. I had never heard or read in the logbooks of anyone bushwhacking cross-country over that terrain to get to Goat Haunt Ranger Station. I figured I could possibly find a route, even if I had to get off course by many miles. This would take hunting and pecking along the course, to the crest of the ridge saddle, to discover a successful way. This basin is also prime grizzly habitat, as park biologists had informed me, although I had never encountered one near that range. Fortunately, most bears were in hibernation mode at the time and would likely not be out-and-about that late in the fall.

Goat Haunt Ranger Station closed on October 10, at the end of tourist and fishing season. My pursuers would not be expecting me to trek that way, by this cross-country route. Someone would likely be at Stoney Indian Pass to stop me at that passageway. However, if I were careful and quick enough, I could sneak past the searchers on my way to Kaina Creek, then work my way up the creek bed and take the fork that runs out of White Crow Basin. Then, I could bushwhack across the basin to the base of the cliff-like ridge. Kaina creek bed would be the quickest and easiest route into that cirque.

I was not very familiar with White Crow Basin, as it lies off the beaten path. I had bushwhacked my way into the area two years ago, just to see what I could see, and just because it was there. It was a beautiful area to poke around in. It was green and lush, with poplar and birch trees, bracken ferns, snowberries, alder, devils club, elder-berries, mountain ash and huckleberries, and a few conifers mingled in here and there. These berries are a favorite food of both species of bruin, throughout the northwest.

I had backtrailed about a mile down the valley when I heard a fast paced horseman coming from behind. I was not using the hiking trail. I had kept off the trails, as I would be leaving tracks, and could be exposed in many open places. It was slow going, moving through the brush, but I was safer. The rider passed at a lope, as I lay low in the bushes. I was sure the desperado who passed would be communi-cating with the rest of the hunting party about what had happened, and who was dead. With men likely waiting at both of the passes, the others were still combing the valley where they had shot that first elk. Conceivably, they could be trying to flush me out to one of the guarded passes or road exits. I still had no indication how many of them there were. Positively, there was one less man. The rest would be desperate to find me and terminate me, out of pure vengeance.

At the moment, I felt safe and needed to stop and dress my wound. I had no idea how bad it was. I removed my pack, retrieved the first aid kit, removed my shirts and cleaned the wound as best I could with what little gauze I had and with the help of a clean bandana. In my kit was a small vile of iodine that I dribbled on the wound. That burned me and made my eyes water from the stinging drops. With a roll of adhesive tape and a couple of fresh gauze pads, I taped over the area after adding a liberal amount of Neosporin directly on the wound. I replaced my shirts and worked on the horse cinch to make a sling for the rifle. I sliced each end of the cinch with my knife, lengthwise, about eight inches from each end. This gave me two strands still married together at one end. Then I tied one end around the forearm, and I tied the other end around the stock behind the rifle's lever, beyond the pistol grip. I could carry it across my good shoulder and have both hands free.

I progressed down the valley toward Cosley Lake to the back-country campground, as the search party slowly rode up the valley toward me. I needed a hiding place fast, before I ran into them face-to-face.

Cosley Lake Campground is situated on the west shore of the lake near where Kaina Creek enters the lake's outlet. A short distance beyond the campground is semi-open meadowland, scattered with limber pines growing on small, rolling, open knolls. There is grass for ground cover, but no brush for cover, along those hogbacks. This was too much exposure for me to risk being caught. I decided to stay back by the campground where there was much more shrubbery and thick cover. A typical backcountry campsite has one outhouse, which is shared by both males and females. For some unknown reason, Cosley Lake Campground has two privies. This particular campground has five fire grates, which means a maximum of twenty campers can camp there, due to the permit reservation system the Park employs. The shadow of a plan for my hideaway began forming in my mind.

One privy is closer to the campsite and is used the most by overnighters, due to its close proximity and quick access. The other privy is a little farther from the camp, in the brush and trees. It is partially visible from the campground. Park backcountry outhouses are built to last for many years. First, a pit is dug into the ground, six feet deep and four feet square. Three-inch thick and twelve-inch wide rough-sawn boards, four feet long, are stacked edge-to-edge and end-to-end with the ends spiked together at the lapped corners. This board stacking continues until the cribbing is as deep as the hole, and the finished height is barely higher than the surface grade of the ground. The space around the outside of the cribbing is then back-filled with the excess dirt from the pit diggings. The outhouse floor is constructed atop the cribbing; the walls are erected, the rafters are built and the exterior 1"x 6" applied. Finally, there's the roofing mate-rial, and a door is made for entry.

It had been over an hour since the shooting. I crept into the semi-open campground area, and then moved cautiously to the lakeshore; where I glassed the shorelines and the meadow to the north, with its scattered limber pines, for my enemies on horseback. Quickly I spotted a poacher traveling toward the foot of the lake, riding into the beginning of the grassy, hogback meadows. I needed to hide quickly. The searching terminators would have to split up, with half of the cutthroats taking the east side of the lake and the remainder searching the westside shoreline, through the campground and behind it. With only four traveling in my direction, it lessened the odds against me if shots were fired. I'd be dealing with four-to-one odds in a shootout. I hoped nothing remotely like that would happen. I didn't like those odds or having to shoot someone else, unless neces-sary. What if I became pinned down? That would give the others time to come to a firefight from the other side of the lake. Then I'd be toast for sure.

I ran to the farthest outhouse from the camp, where there was more cover. I got a harebrained idea; I would hide in the outhouse basement. I grabbed a handful of some small, dead and down branches, bark and ground duff. I dropped them into the outhouse hole through the seat opening. This base would keep me from sinking into whatever might still be down there that had not decomposed since summer. I repeated the process until I had a firm base at the bottom of the pit. I climbed down into the dregs through the seat opening. I could almost stand up straight, but needed another six inches of pit depth to accommodate my six-foot seven-inch height. The pit didn't stink because chlorinated lime had been sprinkled frequently into the hole throughout the summer months. Lime speeds up the decomposing process. There was very little odor, other than a faint chlorine smell.

Suddenly I felt very stupid. In my panic to hide, I had cornered myself and had only one way out. If I were discovered here, this pit toilet would become my grave, making it easy for them to dispose of me. Only my murderers would ever know where my body was laid to rest. I am sure I'd be the topic of a joke between them for many years, if they succeeded with my death in this toilet's waste-hole tomb. It was too risky to climb out and find another hiding place. There wasn't time.

I did have a clear vantage point from there, though. I could see out in all directions through the wide gaps between the top of the cribbing and the floor joists. The gaps gave me enough space to fire the rifle horizontally with some latitude, in all directions. I'd be able to take a few of them with me if a gunfight started. They wouldn't immediately know from where the shots were fired. The element of surprise would be my only benefit in firing from this dugout. I was still trapped and outnumbered. Evening up the odds would be helpful before others arrived to help, but I doubted my ability to survive in the end.

Moments later, I saw two riders approaching the campground, just minutes after I had climbed into the hole. One rider would pass between the lake and me. The others would pass between me, and the area behind the outhouse. I watched nervously as I wondered what they would do when they neared the outhouses. I hoped that none of them would have to relieve themselves. Again, I was trying to see their faces for identification and also any brands on their mounts. The rider nearest to the lakeshore was the one that shot me in the shoulder. The saddle was partially repaired, with the reins from the dead horse's bridle used as a cinch. The straps were doubled up for more width. "Damn, I should have cut the 'D' rings from the saddle," I thought. "Then it would be almost impossible for them to saddle up." The guy's rifle was scoped. If there was shooting, I'd take him out first, and then quickly shoot the second man.

As the manhunters approached the outhouse area, one yelled, "Hey, what about checking the crappers?" "Why? Well, Okay," the other replied."I'll check them, but he wouldn't be dumb enough to hide in one of those, eh?"

As he walked nearer, my heart pounded out of my chest. I was sure he could hear its rhythmic beat. I wondered to what extent he would be checking. I could see the man who shot at me walking toward the first outhouse, pistol in hand. He opened the door, then stepped back and let it slam shut. Then he proceeded toward my possible tomb.

He walked casually, which gave me the feeling he thought this was a ridiculous waste of time, but should probably be done anyway.

I shifted on my haunches with the rifle aimed at the opening in the stool seat. If he happened to look in the hole, the last thing he'd see would my face, and the blast from the muzzle of the barrel. I would have no choice but to fire, and then quickly fire a shot at the other guy. These men were looking to kill me. Naturally, I'd rather they be killed than I. Surprise would be on my side for the first shot, and possibly for the second.

The door opened. I was temporarily blinded by the daylight that flooded in. I saw no shadows moving above me. The door seemed to stay open for many minutes although I am sure the time was brief. "Let it slam shut, please," I thought. In a second or two, the light faded and the door slapped shut, with the long coil spring giving a "twang" sound as it closed. Phew! Then, I felt I had to relieve myself. I was certainly in the right place for that. That feeling quickly faded as I saw him mount his horse and continue the search. The other riders slowed their pace to let him catch up.

I waited for a few minutes, and climbed out as quietly as I could from my stoop. I left the campground through the thickest cover I could find, heading for Kaina Creek. When I arrived at the creek, I washed my hands and face, and then ate a sandwich that I had taken from their saddlebags. It was almost one o'clock in the afternoon. I rechecked my wound and made sure the bandage was still secure and remained dry. I was blessed, it was a shallow surface wound but it did hurt. I knew it would be many more days before it scabbed over and knitted back together.

5

At Kaina Creek, I began my upward climb, staying on the edge of the creek bank where it was dry. I needed to make it to the summit of the saddle between Mt. Cleveland and Kaina Mountain before 5 p.m., and descend the other side while there was still enough sunlight to see my way down safely.

I needed daylight to get over and beyond the summit. Autumn daylight hours shrink noticeably shorter each day. Climbing this ridge at night could mean certain death, and spending the night at these elevations could kill a man with the bitter cold, frost and breezes. I had only my down vest, medium-weight jacket and a small, thin space blanket. That was not enough to ward off the bitter temperatures all night long. If the wind kicked up, it would suck the heat right out of my body and I'd freeze to death quickly. There is always a slight breeze at higher elevations due to the convection of heat from the day. Air currents travel up the slopes during the day and down at night. This is the rule in the mountains.

The farther I continued up the creek, the brushier the terrain became along the creek bank. I finally decided to walk in the center of the slippery creek. My toes soon became numb from the icy water, but hiking there was faster than fighting the brush along the creek bank.

I finally began approaching close to the basin; the ground opened up with less foliage than what I had been climbing through. The vegetation transitioned into occasional coniferous trees, a few quaking aspens and a variety of low-growing shrubs. Farther ahead, the vegetation petered out as the talus and cliffs began to rise sharply to the base of Mt. Cleveland, along the ridge that married into Mt. Kaina. It was imperative that I ascend this knifelike ridge before nightfall. The climb to the ridge top would be close to fifteen hundred feet in elevation, with no man-made trail to follow.

I left the creek as soon as the foliage thinned, and headed southwest across the basin toward the talus that leads upward from the cliffs' base below the summit. I was at least three miles from the nearest member of the search party, and none of them would be following me.

I thought to myself, "What a day this has been." In just 10 hours' time, I had been shot at, wounded, chased, stalked, and I had killed a man. This was like a movie, or a bad dream, but it was real, and happening in the here-and-now. This was a dream I couldn't wake from.

I saw movement. Then, I saw them. It was a grizzly sow with two cubs meandering toward me, a safe distance away. I thought, "Why hasn't she and her cubs denned up by now?" I hadn't seen tracks of a bear in the valley floor for weeks. At the moment she had no notion I was in the area, but she would likely catch my scent soon enough.

Every grizzly is potentially dangerous, but a sow with cubs becomes more aggressive and dangerous. A sow's maternal instinct is to protect her young at all costs. A sow with cubs is often the cause of maulings and deaths, but not all occur this way. Grizzlies have no natural enemies other than Man, and they don't fear him when cubs are involved. I've never seen a grizzly with cubs spook and run off when surprised by a man, like a black bear might do sometimes. Black bears have killed more people in the Continental United States than grizzlies have. But there are fewer grizzlies than black bears, so the statistics speak for themselves. A sow's sole mission is protection of her cubs. This creates unpredictable results, as she is prone to charge in order to maim, kill or otherwise deter danger away from her young.

These two teddy bear cubs looked to be that spring's young. They both weighed in the forty to fifty pound range. At that age, the sow's sole mission is to maintain the cubs' safety. Soon they will be in hibernation. I wished they had already bedded down for the winter. This state of affairs was just bad luck and timing.

I stood motionless, checking for a close tree to climb, while keeping an eye on momma, to see when she would catch my scent. Unfortunately, she was moving downwind from me. In a matter of moments, she'd know I was within her maternal protection zone. My scent would be strong, as I had perspired heavily throughout the day, and of course, there was the scent of blood from my shoulder wound. I'd picked a tree close enough to climb quickly, if she decided to charge. Adult grizzlies cannot climb trees due to their mitten-shaped hands. Young grizzly cubs have paws with fingers, until they mature out of that stage into adulthood. The cubs can climb trees for protection, only while they are young. It is their sole defense.

Black Bears can climb trees, as they have fingers like humans, for gripping. Therefore, if a bear climbs up a tree after you, it's a black bear and if it knocks the tree down, it's a grizzly.

The sow's head lifted suddenly as she sniffed the air, and then directed her focus toward me. She stood looking ahead, trying to locate and identify the scent that threatened her territory. Immediately, she dropped down on all fours with a commanding woof to her young cubs. Both cubs quickly scurried up a nearby tree.

I slung my rifle over my shoulder and mimicked what the cubs did. She charged directly toward me in a dead run from 70 yards away. Her large body crashed through the small underbrush, like she was on a string that was fastened to me. I climbed as fast and far up the tree as I could, about 12 feet above the ground. I was nestled in a medium lodgepole pine. My adrenaline kicked in and launched me up the tree faster than usual. This species of tree usually doesn't have many branches at the base so I shinnied my way up like I was climbing a pole. Some hikers have encountered a charging grizzly and climbed a tree with a few lower branches, only to find the bear also stepped on those same branches and was able to reach up and pull them from the tree. I was safe at the height I had attained.

At the trunk of my tree, she stopped and stood up, with both paws reaching up at me. She pushed against the tree, which didn't shake. She clawed at the air while reaching and trying to grab me; I was easily five feet above her large talons. She soon dropped to all fours and circled the tree while she stared a hole in me.

My shoulder began throbbing, and I knew by the warmth that it was bleeding again. My bearhug around the tree took considerable effort and energy, and was straining my upper arms and shoulders.

She circled the tree a few times, sat a few feet from the trunk and continued to glare at me. I made myself more comfortable by shinnying up a mite higher, to support my thighs on a couple of smaller, broken branch stubs that were poking out from the trunk.

My wristwatch was moving in slow motion, and the minutes dragged by. Thirty minutes had elapsed before she finally gave up and moseyed back to her treed cubs. She gave a guttural command; it was time for the cubs to return to earth. As the cubs reached the ground, she sniffed them over till she was satisfied they were all right, and they resumed their journey as if my intrusion had never occurred. She likely figured I was no threat to her young and decided to leave.

I hung on to my tree in a tree-hugger death grip a while longer. I was exhausted and grateful the sow hadn't been more persistent in our stalemate. I wasn't sure how much longer I could have hung on, but fear is a great motivator when it demands one to hang on for their life. I watched the three bears until they vanished, then slid down the tree to sit on the ground against the trunk to relax for a few minutes more and let my muscles rejuvenate.

Opening my pack, I searched for my first aid kit to re-dress my wound. The blood was starting to cake and had oozed down and soaked through the front of my uniform shirt; I mopped my skin with the old bandage and repatched it with fresh materials. I took a moment to eat the apple and the last peanutbutter bar, since I knew I would need some energy for the upward scale out of the basin and over the saddle. The bear incident had stolen precious time. I needed to gain ground toward the cliffs and up to the summit. I needed to hurry my pace so as not to be climbing over the precipice in the dusk or darkness.

6

Quickly, I was on my feet to begin climbing the talus to the rock cliffs above. I'd lost almost an hour of daylight with the bear incident and needed those minutes to hunt and peck the best route on the cliffs above. I did not want to become cliff-bound and then have to backtrack, wasting more daylight and energy. I calculated the best possible route, using my field glasses, checking out any route that appeared promising.

At high elevations in the park, mountain sheep and mountain goats spend their days browsing for food. These ungulates use the ridges and cliffs to traverse from mountain to mountain on their byways, daily. Mountain goats travel along ledges on the cliffs that are narrow, wide or steep. This is their normal routine, and their balance is unmatched in the animal kingdom. In past cross-country foot patrols, I have encountered a number of these rugged, natural goat trails that are quite safe for human foot travel. Normally these paths become extremely steep, precariously dangerous and unsafe for human travel. Some ledges encounter dangerous cliff exposures, with drop-offs of hundreds of feet, or narrow paths less than a foot wide. Mountain goats are ballerinas upon these narrow rock formations, and continue to live long lives. In the end, they eventually die from attacks by mountain lions or bears, from hunters or from avalanches. The very old eventually perish from falls, as they lose their balance with old age. On some ledges, I had to get down on all fours to mimic the height of a goat. Rock overhangs might extend out above these goat paths, making it impossible to stand. Then one must crawl along on the trail until they can stand again. The overhangs don't faze goats, because a goat's shoulder has no connection to their main skeletal structure, like human bodies have. This enables them to get their bodies down low and to worm their way through areas impossible for humans to go.

My favorite goat trail is not marked on any park service map. This trail is described in a few hiking and climbing guidebooks. Goat trails are recommended for travel only by experienced hikers, in good health and physical condition. This particular trail is above the Ptarmigan Tunnel and travels north to Red Gap Pass. In some places, it's wider than a concrete sidewalk, and is very safe from exposure. The trail also travels south to Iceberg Notch and Ahern Pass. This trail is full of exposure and the winds can play havoc with one's balance. The views are incredible, to say the least. Sometimes a hiker will run face-to-face into goats meandering toward him. When a goat encounters a hiker, it immediately turns tail and scurries back on the trail or climbs to another trail above or below, where we bipeds could never safely follow. Most of the time, they instantly vanish among the rocks and cliffs, without a trace.

Goat trails can be a good, safe way to travel through the high country, especially if one's destination is to climb a peak or to travel cross-country to another trail. I needed a trail like that to gain elevation safely, to the ridge top.

Finding a goat trail is as simple as finding goats along the rocky cliffs. They traverse these ledges in search of food or for protection from predators. In late afternoon hours, goats are generally looking for a place to bed down for the night, in the safety of the cliffs. The mountain beyond Kaina is in fact named Goat Haunt Mountain due to the large population of goats that haunt this mountain throughout the year. My destination was the headwaters of Waterton Lake, on the

U.S. side of Canada's Waterton Park. Goat Haunt Ranger Station is planted at the base of Goat Haunt Mountain.

With my binoculars, I located a couple of white spots on the rock cliff above me. They were definitely goats traversing the basin cliff face that I was about to climb. These goats were migrating from Mt. Cleveland (the tallest mountain peak in the park) toward Kaina Mountain. I watched their migration to landmark a possible route to their footpath. I needed a course that would marry up to that same avenue of travel. I found a runoff chute that would take me there. It looked promising; and the only artery that looked achievable. Climbing up to that junction, I might see different possibilities to continue on safely. A large portion of the ground below the wall-like ridge was talus, of fist-size and smaller red, flat shale, called red or brown argillite.

I was in a rush to get to the ridge, as daylight was beginning to fade and the shadows were growing longer in the valley below. I began upward on the steep talus which made noise as the loose rocks shifted under my boots. When stepping forward, I would slide backward half a step. This continued with every step. Climbing talus is slow, exhausting work. The gravelly hillside is still safer than climbing the cliffs though, which I would be scaling soon enough. Finally, I was approaching the talus slope's apex inception, where the cliffs rise steeply upward to the ridge skyline. Reaching this summit, I continued upward in a steep, dry, run-off chute, where I began using all fours for climbing and balance. I was gaining elevation quickly.

My rifle was slung over my good shoulder, which became a nuisance and was cumbersome. I wondered if I should discard the carbine. I didn't know if I would have a use for it any longer. Besides, I still had my pistol. The rifle stock banged against the sides of the rocky chute in this narrow hallway, with each footstep and arm-hold forward. The offbeat rhythm of the gunstock bouncing against my side, hip and the rocks was annoying. It was like having a small stone in my boot. My nagging subconscious told me to hang on to the rifle. It's a fact, "If there is going to be shooting, always take a rifle." I decided I would keep it until it became unsafe for me to carry.

As I progressed upward, I kept searching for any achievable route to the goat trail above me. I had gained considerable elevation and had to rest, and continue looking ahead. I glanced down at the basin to see what progress I had made. I was not able see the ridge crest above me. The steepness of the erect, rocky wall I faced blocked my view. There was no movement down below me. I was convinced that my predators would never consider this cross-country route.

I stood below the ridge where the growing afternoon shadows were stretching eastward quickly and dragging the temperature lower. The sun was still shining on the west side and would set into its nighttime gloom in less than two hours. My daylight was disappearing. I needed the sun's light to see my way down the west side of the mountain.

I had accomplished a third of the distance up the cliff face when I finally came upon a ledge where goats traveled. There was old, and fresh, goat scat on the byway, so it was quite obvious they walked there regularly. The air was cooling quickly, so I grabbed my down vest from the pack and put it over my sweat-soaked uniform shirt. A light breeze made it seem colder than it actually was. In my sweat-drenched state, I could feel the heat being sucked out of me. Even though I was struggling and burning up lots of energy, I was chilled. Temperatures drop quickly at this altitude and would soon plunge below freezing.

I trudged along the goat trail as it gradually ascended toward Mt. Cleveland. I was situated midway between the two mountains, climbing southward. A hundred steep yards later, the trail cut back toward Kaina. It had become so steep I was using my cold hands and numb fingers to grip the frigid rocks, to climb and to keep my balance. My fingers felt like marbles trying to grip the chilled and abrasive rocks.

I was sweating profusely under my vests inside lining. Nevertheless, I was warmer, as the vest's 60/40 shell broke the breeze blowing on my back and sides. I was burning a lot of energy, straining and pulling my 220-pound frame and backpack upward. My stomach was empty; I hadn't had much to eat, for all the distance I had traveled since dawn. I had hiked many miles of territory since this all began this morning. My energy and adrenaline were drained. I was exhausted, but not beat. I imagined I'd accomplished twenty-five miles off-trail, with a hefty amount of elevation gain thus far. Twelve hours had passed since breakfast, which included a couple of fried eggs with toast, butter and honey. Since then, I had consumed only two peanutbutter bars, a sandwich and an apple. I was sure my stomach thought my throat had been cut.

I stopped on a ledge, put down my pack and took out a packet of dried Gatorade. I added that to my canteen, shook it up and drank half the liquid before stopping. When I reached the summit, I would eat my little can of tuna. I knew I'd feel better with something in my boiler room. I put my gear back into the pack and continued up the breeze-chilled exposure.

I arrived at the summit on a lower saddle just after five o'clock, and the sun was closing its eye behind the western horizon. I only backtrailed once when I became cliff-bound. Darkness was closing in. I looked back down from where I had come; it was almost night time in the valley far below. The shadows had smeared together in the lowlands. On the west side there was still enough fading light to find my way down if I moved quickly. Immediately, I dropped down to another goat trail and began trekking downhill toward the talus. I had to get off the cliffs before I was no longer able to see safely. Soon I'd be careening down the talus slopes below, dropping elevation in short order.

The western side of the ridge wasn't as steep as the east side. Storms enter from the west. creating more erosion on the windward western side, breaking down the cliffs over a period of many centuries. Farther below, a long, wide talus slope stretched downward to the timberline. Once on the talus, I could descend to the timber in short order.

I left the rocky face and stepped onto the talus. The slope was composed of smaller, golfball-sized rocks. Cascading down this slope turned out to be entertaining. As I stepped outward and down, I slid a few more feet. Each step became magnified through this slide. With a slow, walk-trot, I was surfing down the slope in double-time. It was great moving over so much ground with such speed. Finally, something that day was easy. I covered ground to the edge of the timberline in a couple of minutes. At timberline, I began a slow, careful descent down the steep mountainside into thick forest below.

I hadn't eaten my can of tuna at the summit, as planned. I was racing against time to get off the dangerous part of the ridge's backbone while there was still daylight. I stopped and retrieved the tuna can and opened it with my G.I. can opener called a P-38. It is a primitive tool but effective, and quite small. It's a slow process to open can with it. I kept the opener on my key ring that retains my government keys. The P-38 can opener is the same tool our soldiers used during WWII, Korea, and Viet Nam to open their canned rations.

It was just about dark when I began descending a dry creek bed on a very sharp, timbered hillside. The light-colored stones reflected enough light to let me see my way down safely. Stepping cautiously, I had to take care to keep my balance and footing from sliding, tumbling, and falling.

I could see a few of the roofs of the ranger station complex, two miles to the north. Farther along were the lights of Canada's Waterton Town Site, at the opposite end of the eight-mile-long lake. Waterton Lake is situated on both sides of the forty-ninth parallel. My descent was painstaking slow, as I was creeping down the declining creek bed. As I closed in on the valley floor, the available light darkened by a few shades. The large stand of Engleman spruce that lives in the moist, lush bottomland of Valentine Creek grows thick, full crowns, blocking out considerable light. Even during the daytime, the light is softer. I continued downward in the creek runoff channel, where it became quite dangerously vertical in places. Skirting the drop-offs ate up a lot time and was aggravating to me in my fatigued state.

7

The mountainside finally began leveling out near the valley floor. It was darker than nighttime should be, under this tent of hemlock and spruce branches. I pulled my little Mag-Lite from my pack and picked my way through the blowdowns to the Valentine Creek Trail. Once on the trail, the hike became effortless, on that level and well-maintained path.

Pushing the button on my watch for illumination, I could see it was almost seven o'clock. I wasn't far from the station. The temperature had dropped to below freezing. I put my jacket on and kept my rifle handy, in case I happened to run into another bear or maybe an outlaw. Not that I'd be able to see anything or even aim to shoot, but it gave a comfortable sense of security having it handy. Our minds do funny things when we are in the dark. One begins to imagine all sorts of images of dangers that lurk there. When alone and in the dark, we have an element of self-inflicted, imaginary fear, with our indistinct surroundings and the concealed predator that is not really there.

Arriving at the station's housing hamlet, I was alert to carefully check the surrounding area for any sign of other persons being there. After creeping around looking for tracks and listening, I decided there was no evidence of anyone else was in the immediate area. I saw no horse- or man-tracks on the dirt walkways.

I went directly to the station's main office and unlocked the door, after first removing the bear door. Entering the office, I felt around for the supply cabinet lock and keyed it open. Reaching in, I searched for the shelf where a large flashlight was usually kept. My flashlight's batteries had gone dead a few minutes before.

This ranger station, in the summer months, serves as the sub-district headquarters for the Goat Haunt Sub-District, which includes the Belly River drainages. Therefore, I am quite familiar with the buildings and the grounds.

Finding the flashlight and switching it on, I took a quick look around the office. The radio wasn't there. It must have been removed for the winter, to be checked over by the park's electronics shop. There were no handsets available either. The large batteries for the main radio were all that remained. This station used a diesel generator for electricity. The generator ran daily, in the mornings and evenings, for the use of the park employees that were stationed there seasonally. It also recharged the radios' batteries. The staff consisted of three rangers, two naturalists and a trail crew of four, for this portion of the sub-district.

I chose to spend the night in the office, as opposed to using the employees' quarters. The closet storeroom had all the necessities I needed: sleeping bags, blankets, a foam mattress pad, MRE rations, a first aid kit, matches and a Coleman lantern, among other items. I was looking forward to a good night's rest. When tomorrow arrived, I'd decide how best to proceed in this fiasco. I retrieved a foam ground pad and sleeping bag, and spread both on the floor. I pulled the bear door shut and closed the office door. I locked the latter for some reason, as if that would stop something or somebody from entering, if they really decided to join me. I grabbed a bag of MRE rations, wrapped up in a blanket and sat at the desk, to eat a cold package of spaghetti with meatballs, dehydrated peaches, and dessert of a small, vacuum-sealed portion of pound cake. I washed it down with my canteen water with the Gatorade in it.

I removed my jacket, vest, shirt, pistol and holster, boots and socks, and then slid into the down-filled bag. After turning off the lantern, I don't even recall my head resting against the sleeping bag, as I instantly fell into a deep, exhausted sleep.

I awoke with a start, with the morning light streaming in through the small, horizontal cracks in the office shutters. I sat up, trying to clear my head, and rubbed the sleep from my eyes. My watch face declared it was almost eight. I got up slowly and found my shoulder was stiff and sore from yesterday's injury. Other parts of my body made me aware I still had a body. With each movement, the muscles moaned that they were still tired. My arms and hands were scratched, scraped and lightly scabbed from climbing up the tree and scrambling over the rocky precipice. However, I was feeling better, having had a good sleep. I was already planning for the day ahead.

I put on my Park Service jacket and the vest over the jacket. The vest had damp spots from yesterday's perspiration. My uniform shirt was stiff with frozen sweat, so I left it draped over the chair until I was leaving. Turning on the battery-powered lantern, I picked up the station daily log diary and looked for the last entries, to find out what happened to the missing radio. I had guessed right, the radio had been removed when the station closed at the end of the season in late September, for replacement parts and upgrades. I made my entry into the logbook, describing yesterday's events and how I got there. I scribbled in today's date and replaced the logbook back on the shelf.

I needed to get moving toward the Town Site, hiking the eight miles north along the western, lakeshore trail. The Park Service boat was in storage at the Town Site for the winter, so that would be of no help to me. I figured I had traveled approximately twenty-eight miles through rough terrain yesterday and was not looking forward to hiking the trail today, even if it was an easy, level walk. This was just one more thing I needed to do to in order to contact Saint Mary Station, to get assistance and inform them of yesterday's felonious activity. The criminals needed to be apprehended while they were still in the area, with the evidence.

Suddenly I heard noises outside, the sound of horse hooves

striking the walkway near the office. I quickly strapped the holster and pistol back on my side and grabbed the rifle. I peeked out between the cracks in the shutters. One of the poachers I had seen yesterday was dismounting a few yards in front of the station office. I spied between other shutter gaps to see if there were additional men with him. I saw nothing and heard no more hooves in the area. I set the rifle down and drew and cocked my pistol.

I had had enough of being hunted, and something snapped within me. I was instantly angry, frustrated, and tired from being hunted and running like an outlaw from a posse. It ticked me off to think that these guys might actually manage to finish me off, get away with this killing escapade and never be caught. Fortunately, I had left an entry in the station daily logbook that addressed the situation. It would be of some real help to the investigation that would take place if the Park Service came looking for me and I wasn't found. I unlocked the door quietly and pulled it inward. I stepped in front of the closed bear door. Through the cracks in the shutters, I could see where my assassin was standing. Lifting my left foot, I kicked the door outward and followed behind it through the opening, jumping down from the office step to the ground. My executioner jerked around, startled, with a surprised expression. As he focused on me, his left hand grabbed the forearm and began lifting the rifle toward me. My pistol was already aimed and cocked, and I was ready to squeeze the trigger if things went south.

"Don't!" I yelled, but his rifle kept swinging upward to shoot. I fired twice, so fast that it almost sounded like one shot. Two holes appeared near the "V" where his jacket collar came together at breast height. He buckled backward over a stone planter and remained still on the dirt walkway. He had been less than 30 feet away. He could have shot from his hip faster at that distance, with a better chance of hitting me than taking the time to sight aim.

8

I made ready to leave for the Town Site immediately. The shots would be heard at quite a distance, with the mountains echoing the thundering blasts. There was no way of telling if others were in the area, so I needed to get out of there immediately. I closed and locked the station door behind me after grabbing my personals, pack and rifle. I had to run in case others were close and racing toward this destination. I decided to steal the dead man's horse. I figured he didn't have a use for it any longer. I mounted up and loped to the trail that leads to the Town Site. I slowed my pace at the lake trail and let the horse walk across the ford at the river's inlet. Once on the other bank, I loosened the reins so the horse could again lope along at a comfortable pace. After a quarter mile, I stopped and adjusted the stirrups to fit my long legs. If there happened to be more outlaws in the area, they would be hurrying to, or already be at, the station. My thoughts went back to the man I had just shot. I tried to piece together how he might have gotten there this morning. He was on horseback, which meant he had to have come over Stoney Indian Pass and then down to Pass Creek and continue on to the Valentine Creek Trail. He would have had to hole up someplace along the trail for the night, and then continue down Valentine Creek Trail to the station this morning. He had likely broken away from the others after they passed by me while I hid in the outhouse. When the search team was unsuccessful at the head of the valley, he must have decided to ride over the pass on the chance that I had gone to the Goat Haunt Ranger Station by another way, or that I had slipped by them somehow. If he had not spent the night on the trail, we both would likely have arrived at the station at about the same time. That would not have been a comforting thought for me, especially in the dark.

I was four miles from the Canadian border. As I rode closer, I could see the border swath, which cuts a cleared corridor between the two countries. I knew I had to be cautious; there could be one more sentry at the border watching for my exit into Canada.

I inspected the dirt and the iced-over puddles on the trail for any sign that someone had already passed that way. I slowed the horse to a walk, to make the investigation easier. I saw nothing that led me to believe anyone else had used the trail recently. There were no signs of horse travel or anything else telling. The swath between the two countries is easy to see. The border commission keeps the trees cleared in the 20-foot wide laceration of the 49th parallel. The swath is a treeless span extending from Lake Superior to Vancouver, along the friendly, Canada-United States border.

Just before reaching the border, I eased up on the horse's pace, dismounted and led him on foot. I figured someone who had set up an ambush there could shoot me. I had no way to tell what might be in store ahead. I attempted to be as watchful as possible; unfortunately, my horse made it easy to spot my presence. I was blessed with good cover along the trail, to duck into, if I was shot at and missed. If I was shot at and killed, then nothing would matter anyway; it would be over and they would be free men, having terminated my existence. In that case, the daily logbook I left would be helpful to seize those clowns later.

I passed through the boundary swath border, leading the horse without incident. I was officially in Canada. My entry was illegal, since I was packing a pistol. Pistols are unlawful to possess in any Canadian province. I also had a loaded rifle, but under the circumstances, I didn't shiv-a-get. My Park Service badge meant nothing there, concerning law enforcement activities. The pistol was just plain illegal in Canada. I was taking a chance that, considering my predicament, the pistol wouldn't warrant any legal infractions from the Canadian Government. I honestly didn't imagine they would arrest me under these circumstances. I was banking on that.

I remounted and loped along toward the Town Site at a very comfortable gait. The horse was a good mountain horse, handled with ease to neck reining and was quick to react to the gentle prod of my boot heels. Whether at a trot or at a lope, this animal had a real smooth gait and seemed content to stay at whatever pace I commanded. The chestnut was very well disciplined, had good muscle tone and conformation as far as I could tell, beneath his heavy winter coat.

I was enjoying the ride after yesterday's death hunt to stay alive. I felt that any remaining danger was behind me. The Town Site was less than a mile away. I was making good time on horseback.

At the city limits, I reined the mount straight down Main Street. No one was active that morning, and it dawned on me that it was Sunday. I passed boarded-up gift shops, stores, vacant motels and cafes, reminders that the tourist season was over for the year, and the town had been placed into hibernation for the winter.

A population of approximately seventy people lived in town during the long winter months. In summer, the population exploded to make it a very busy tourist town. Just then, it appeared to be a ghost town.

At the end of the street, I reined the horse toward the police station. The station's hanging porch sign read, "Royal Canadian Mounted Police." The building appeared to be more of a cute cottage than a law enforcement establishment. This station included two Mounties working shifts, splitting the day and night shifts between themselves, during the winter months. In summer, there were two additional law enforcers stationed there.

I rode up to the front of the station; I dismounted and tied the reins to the small yard's picket fence in front. After removing the rifle from the scabbard, I stepped up the flagstoned path to the front porch. The sign on the door read "ENTER," so I turned the knob and walked in.

A male about my age, in his late twenties or very early thirties, was seated behind the desk to the right of the door across the room. He stared me in the eye as I crossed the room toward him. I knew he was focused on my rifle and pistol. He wasn't able to see my Park Service badge or jacket emblem clearly, as my vest was covering them.

I laid the rifle on his desk and said, "I am a Park Service Ranger in Glacier National Park and I've had some serious trouble." I removed the vest and backed up to the fireplace where a good bed of coals was throwing off some welcomed heat. That's when he saw my badge. The Mountie said nothing, but continued to watch at me with concern.

As I removed my jacket I said, "I was shot yesterday morning by poachers while on duty in the Belly River Drainage. I am in need of medical attention, as you can see. I also need to get word to Saint Mary Ranger Station about the crimes involved. The poachers are still in the valley searching for me.

His eyes changed, registering excitement, when he saw my bandaged shoulder, with the dried, caked blood around the lump of gauze, and on my shirt. He quickly jumped up and headed for the door. "I'll get you a doctor for that wound. I'll be right back."

I wasn't planning on going anywhere at the moment, anyway. The heat from the fire felt too good to part from. The gentleman left through a side door. I wondered if he had any food handy, as I hadn't eaten since the previous night. I was as hungry as a spring bear out of hibernation.

He returned rather quickly with another man following close behind him carrying a leather bag. "This is our town doctor, Dr.Higgs."

"Hi, pleased to meet you. I hope I am not disturbing you this morning," I said.

"Seriously, young man, this is not a problem," said Dr. Higgs.

"Take that shirt all the way off and have a seat in this chair by the fire. I've been somewhat bored, with nothing to do since the season ended, and I very seldom see gunshot wounds. So this is most interesting for me."

I shed my uniform shirt and tee shirt to expose my shoulder. Dr. Higgs peeled my crude bandages off, with the soiled and dried blood, to inspect the wound. I looked up as the Mountie was introducing himself. "I am Eric Stewart. I'd really like to hear your story of what happened yesterday and how you ended up here this morning." I, in turn, introduced myself to Eric and to Dr. Higgs. I hesitated for a moment about the story, as Eric was the law north of the border, but then I figured, "What the heck. It would pass some time while I warmed up by the fire and the Doctor worked his magic on my wound." Both men were curious about what had happened, so I gave them a quick synopsis of what had transpired since yesterday morning's first gunshot. They both listened intently as I explained the events in the order of their occurrence. When I finished, I asked if there was some eatery still open where I could buy breakfast.

Dr. Higgs spoke up, "When I am finished cleaning this wound and patching you up, I'd like both of you to come with me to my home for brunch. My wife is in the process of preparing a meal at this moment, and we have plenty enough to eat. Please join us; you're more than welcome to dine with us."

When the gray-haired doctor had finished his handiwork, he said, "I believe brunch is probably close to being ready. Come along, I am sure we can fill you both up with a good, hot Sunday meal." We left through the side door, with the good doctor leading the way, as Stewart and I tagged along. Dr. Higgs's home was of European design with Dutch hipped rooflines, and gingerbread trim everywhere on the exterior. This dollhouse was painted red and white, similar to the looks of a barn, but more like something out of a Goldilocks storybook. The house was beautiful and well maintained and decorated, gingerbread-like home.

When we entered, Dr. Higgs introduced me to his wife and said that we both would be staying for brunch. Mrs. Higgs smiled and seemed grateful to have guests for Sunday brunch. She placed two more sets of plates and utensils on the table. Stewart and I sat down where the places had been set.

After saying grace, we began eating. Eric started asking many more questions about the situation I had encountered yesterday, and what happened this morning. Dr. Higgs and his wife listened with intense interest to my responses. You could see the excitement in their eyes as I told the story with much more detail this time.

When we had finished our meal, Stewart said he was willing to help me out. There was no phone service or radio contact available, as last week's storm had downed the phone lines and the radio repeating stations had quit relaying messages. Apparently, it was the same situation on both sides of the border. I needed his cooperation, in case those trophy hunters bailed out of Belly River by way of the old wagon road where it crosses the border into Canada. If they crossed the boundary into Canada, the Park Service and the federal government would have no immediate jurisdiction over them. The process of extradition would be slow and involved. Those marauders needed to be apprehended while they were still in U.S. territory, if possible. Eric Stewart could cover the Canadian side, if they crossed over the border, and nail them for transporting the contraband game meat without them traveling through normal customs inspection. They would be carrying firearms that needed to be legally checked at a border station, also.

I had no knowledge of where the desperados had entered the park or where they might exit. Figuring out where they had left their stock trucks or horse trailers was a guessing game. Did they park near the U.S. Customs station at the trailhead into Belly River? Or, had they driven into the park on reservation land and then crossed the park boundary? They possibly entered on the old mining road that went by Chief Mountain toward Slide Lake. They might have parked near the base of Chief Mountain and rode into the valley by way of the Lee Ridge Trail. I had no other ideas where they might park their rigs. These were the common places where horse parties generally parked, to enter the valley on horseback.

Being faced with all these scenarios, which one should I pursue first? I was sure the poachers were in a quandary, what with two of their party members presently dead. There was a possibility they might not know about the death of the second man at Goat Haunt this morning. They might be expecting his return later in the day. I fully believed they were in an utter frenzy, with the death of the first man near Mokowanis Junction, and frustrated that they had not been able to find and kill me yet. They were frightened for their futures and angered that I was still alive and might have escaped. How would they explain the deaths to the dead men's families and friends? They certainly were in a dilemma, with two of their gang dead.

Maybe the tables had turned, with the poachers realizing that they might be the ones being hunted. They were legal game in the eyes of the law. Once they knew that two of their buddies were dead, they would probably make a run for it, or possibly give themselves up. In their disorganized panic, they could make mistakes and become easier to apprehend, or possibly decide to take a stand and have a final shootout.

I decided to travel to the parking area at the base of Chief Mountain. That was equally distant as the other two potential parking areas. I would be passing by the Customs Trailhead on my way and could investigate that trailhead and the old wagon road from the auto campground on the Canadian side into Belly River.

Would Eric Stewart commit himself to give me a hand with this? "This is a mess," I said. "We have no phone lines, no radio, just flat no communications at all."

Eric said, "The only break you have had in this whole quandary is that you are still alive. Nothing else has been a decent break for you."

All I could do was mutely nod my head in agreement. "Dang! Of all the timing!" I said. "If it can happen, it will," I was thinking. "Murphy's Law is everywhere; when you least expect Murphy, he sneaks in and bites you on the butt."

"Eric, I need a ride to the Chief Mountain Customs buildings where my stock truck is parked. Then, you can return to where the old wagon road exits out of Belly River and crosses the border, in case they head out that way. As you know, the Blood Reservation is a short ways north of the border, and they could have friends there who would take them in. If they come out and cross the border that way, you know what to do. Check them for pistols and transporting game meat across the border," I told him.

"That will work," Stewart said with interest. "Let's get a move on; my truck is parked behind the police station."

We excused ourselves from the table; I thanked the Higgs for the much-needed meal. I had been cooking my own bachelor meals since entering the Belly River Station, at the beginning of June. I had forgotten how good someone else's home cooking could be. A woman's cooking always seems to taste better.

Mrs. Higgs said, "I've got some extra sweet rolls you may take with you for later. I'll put them in a bag to take with you."

"Mrs. Higgs that would be great if you're sure you can spare them," I said gratefully. She handed me a lunch-sack-sized, brown paper bag with warm rolls inside. I could feel the warmth on my hand as I accepted them.

"Nonsense," she said as she dropped a couple more rolls into another bag and handed them to Eric. "I like having an excuse to bake. My husband doesn't eat like he used to, and I love baking in my kitchen."

I thanked her again as I bent down and gave her a peck on the cheek. She was the sweet type of grandma that everyone would have loved to have while growing up. Her face beamed with the peck on her cheek.

"Now you two run along and please be careful," she said as she turned to clear off the table.

"We will try our best to stay out of harm's way, and thanks again for the hot meal and rolls!" I said as I followed Eric out the back door.

Dr. Higgs yelled as the door was closing, "You have that shoulder looked at again as soon as you can."

"You betcha, and thanks for doctoring it up, Doc," I replied, looking back over my shoulder toward him as the door slapped shut.

Stewart and I chewed the fat and brainstormed off the cuff about options and alternative actions we could take. When we entered the office, we headed straight over to the large topographical map on the wall by the fireplace. There, we plotted out all the locations where the poachers' vehicles might be parked. Their exit might have changed and they might have moved their trucks elsewhere if they strongly believed I had made it out of the valley. We decided they might not be doing anything different, other than piling everything into the trucks and making a run for it.

We determined a game plan, which wasn't much of a plan considering there were only two of us to implement it. I asked Stewart if he had a wool shirt I could borrow to put underneath my down vest and jacket. I still had nothing on under my vest. My uniform shirt was still damp and looked a terrible bloody mess. Dr. Higgs had warned me not to wear either a tee shirt or a uniform shirt because of the risk they could cause infection.

Stewart grabbed a shirt out of the entry closet and said, "This is a lost-and-found item, it looks a mite small for you, but I think it will work."

On the inside shirt collar, the tag said "large-tall." I usually wore "extra large-tall." The shirt was long-sleeved, gray wool, medium-weight shirt, like a Pendleton. The shirt happened to be almost the same gray color as my uniform shirt. Trying it on, I found it to be comfortable and only a little snug around the upper chest, and a smidgen short in the sleeves. I pinned the badge from my uniform shirt above the left breast pocket. "This will work," I said. "I am used to ill-fitting clothing: it's a problem that comes with being vertically enhanced. Flat footed, I am five feet and nineteen inches tall. Clothes that fit me correctly are difficult to find, even though I am well-proportioned."

Stewart laughed and said, "Yeah, I bet it's a problem, but I'd still trade you my size for yours, any day."

"No swap," I said smiling. "I enjoy this height, even with all the inconveniences, like finding clothes, long beds and comfortable vehicles, along with low shower heads that are at navel height. There are many situations where I don't fit comfortably. I often bang my head on low doorways, and that hurts big-time. By the way, my tailor is a tent maker." Stewart busted up with laughter.

Eric Stewart stood about five feet and nine inches tall, supporting a very solid-looking, larger-than-average, raw bone frame. He definitely looked like he could handle himself.

9

C anadian Mounties are highly trained in Canadian law and law enforcement techniques. It is difficult to even pass the mental and physical tests to become a Mountie. Under Canadian law, the RCMP can do anything they choose to an individual, to gain control of any particular situation. For example, they can grab someone by the hair or by an ear; use a headlock or an arm bar, anything to gain control and custody. There are no holds barred when a Mountie decides to grasp a situation and gain control. You'll never hear the words "police brutality" north of the border. They are never spoken, because the law backs them up. I knew having a Mountie on my side would be having "one to ride the river with." Eric Stewart was such a man. I was happy to have him along. I hoped he felt the same way about me. Of course, I have not had even a small portion of the training he'd been through, but fortunately, he didn't know that. I was in no wise up to being his equal; considering all the training he had received. I was just big, strong, athletic, very quick, had common sense and was a very good shot.

I put my vest on over the wool shirt, and then the jacket with my other badge still pinned on. Then we walked out to Stewart's four-wheel-drive pickup parked next to the office. As I climbed in, I was immediately aware the vehicle was very well equipped with law enforcement paraphernalia and rescue equipment. A large first aid kit stuck out from under my seat. The pickup bed was covered with a cab-high topper shell. Through the rear window of the cab, I could see some of the bed's contents. The topper and bed were neatly organized, containing enough equipment to equal a tiny sporting-goods store: climbing ropes, a helmet, carabineers, pitons, cross-country skis, a spotting scope, shotgun case, wheel litter, collapsible gurney stretcher, sleeping bag, backpack, rations and such.

We drove out of the Town Site toward the Customs Highway leading to Chief Mountain. It was just past noon when we passed by the only church I saw. The chapel sat upon a small hill near the roadway. The congregation was just leaving the sanctuary's front doors. Folks were clustering together in small groups on the steps and sidewalks, having fellowship with one another after the service ended. While we were passing, a few people waved to the vehicle, which was labeled, "Royal Canadian Mounted Police," on the doors. Townsfolk knew this vehicle by sight, and Stewart responded by lightly tapping on the horn and lifting his open hand above the steering wheel in response to their howdies.

Stewart spoke of his positive feelings toward these friendly residents. "These good people are the folks that live here year around and are our allies and friends. They are good informants when they see something out of place. They treat us like good neighbors and are more than helpful to assist us in our duties."

I agreed. "That's sounds like a perfect situation."

10

Within twenty minutes, we entered the Canadian Parks auto campground known as the Belly River Auto Campground, on the Canadian side of the border. We drove down to where the old wagon road on the Canadian side of Belly River begins its entry into Glacier National Park. This old wagon road exits the park at the border swath, continuing on into Canada. Where it goes from there is a still mystery to me. The wagon road into Belly River no longer exists in its unbroken entirety, due to the 1964 flood washing away many parts of it. The trail was never completely reclaimed after that flood. The log wagon bridge that crossed the river was never rebuilt. Before the flood, Park Service vehicles could drive slowly down the rough wagon road with summer and winter supplies. This was not a regular practice unless it was absolutely necessary. Park policy was very strict about vehicles within the primitive-designated backcountry. The wagon road was used for the Belly River station's horse-and-wagon team to haul in supplies and remove backcountry litter and whatever else needed to be disposed of, from the ranger station. At that time, it existed as a trail-head entry into the valley for hikers, from north of the border. The wagon road was only maintained as a foot trail. Hikers seldom used this trail because they would have to ford the river where the wagon bridge once was. Eric and I saw no evidence that the poachers had entered or left from there. There were no horse tracks or manure. That was obviously not their entry point and they had not left from there.

It was necessary to check this trail to eliminate it as a possible entry point, as it might have been used to enter the valley for their poaching spree, or used as an alternative exit. We drove back to the highway, traveling toward the U.S.-Canadian customs stations. Stewart pulled into an overlook a few miles later that gave a clear view up into the Belly River Valley. He parked the truck at a weird angle, retrieved the spotting scope from the pickup and set it up on the hood. This gave us a direct view up the valley floor.

Stewart motioned, "Here, you know the area and layout better than I. See if you can spot anything. It's aimed to view the center of the valley. The adjusted magnification is sixty power."

I viewed into the valley and was immediately impressed with the scope's clarity. This little beauty was awesome to look through. I scoped the various meadows up the valley and studied them as best I could. Then I began exploring upward toward Lee Ridge and Chief Mountain, for any sort of sign. That yielded no trace of any vehicles, but our elevation was too low to view beyond the top of the ridge. I returned the scope to where I knew a trail should be, in one of the larger meadows. We took turns looking for any movement. Finally, a flickering, twinkling reflection flash caught my eye. We aimed the scope to concentrate our efforts toward that particular meadow. I could make out two riders, each leading two pack animals as they rode across the meadow toward Lee Ridge. After watching for a moment, it was obvious they were parked at the old mining road near the base of Chief Mountain, or at least in that vicinity. The pack-horses were loaded with antlers, capes and, I assumed, the meat. I figured the rest of the posse was still searching for me, in hopes they could still make a clean getaway, leaving me dead, and hiding my remains.

Those renegades were likely planning to get rid of the evidence quickly by selling it or hiding it, making it impossible for anyone to trace and identify that it was from the gut piles left at the kill sites in the park. I needed that wildlife contraband they were going to scurry off with. Viewing only two riders in the scope, I knew there would be more scoundrels at the trucks. With care, Stewart and I might possibly nab those men, before these two desperados arrived to load up and leave.

I had no right to assume Eric Stewart would want to be involved in this situation unless he was willing. I had only presumed he'd join me. I queried, "Eric, would you want to partner up on this situation with me? I know there could be some negative ramifications for you if your government disapproves of your actions, as you would be on the wrong side of the border."

Stewart's expression told the rest of the story. The little crow's-foot wrinkles in the corner of his eyes tightened, as he held back a smile. "Yeah, I'd like in on this, but you need to sign some paperwork saying you're asking for immediate assistance because you're in hot pursuit. Then I'd be considered deputized in your country."

"It's up to my judgment if I decide I want to cross the border and assist." he claimed.

"Well I definitely need your help. If you truly want to partner up, I'll sign whatever you need me to, especially if it keeps you out of hot water with the RCMP."

He quickly grabbed his briefcase, shuffled through the papers and pulled out the forms he needed. After filling out the necessary information, the papers were handed over to me for signing. We then discussed our plan of action to nail these guys. We continued up the road toward the Port of Entry Customs into the U.S. At the locked gate, I jumped out, unlocked it and swung it open for us to pass through to the U.S. side. Then, I closed and locked the gate and jumped back in the truck as we continued down the road toward Chief Mountain.

I began describing the setting and terrain of the area where I expected the stock trucks to be parked. Eric had no knowledge of these grounds across the U. S. border. Where the stock trucks were presumably parked was not actually a formal parking area, but the dead end of the road. It had a huge turnaround area along with a stock-loading ramp. There was plenty of room to park quite a few rigs there. This was a common place for hikers to park to climb Chief Mountain, and a common place for horse parties to enter the Belly River Valley on a less popular hiking trail. Horse parties used this trailhead much more often than backpackers.

11

We turned off the highway onto the dirt, mining road. That unmaintained road is riddled with potholes and icy spots. It was obvious where some heavy trucks had traveled over this road in the recent past. The icy potholes were broken up and had refrozen unevenly, with imprints of large tires in the solidified mud. That told the story that our subjects were likely up this road.

I pointed to a place to park the truck, when we were within a half-mile of the dead end parking area. We were not interested in announcing our arrival by charging straight into the parking area. Stewart backed into the space between some trees and sedimentary boulders, where the vehicle was hidden from passers-by.

"You would have to be looking closely to see this truck now," he said as he closed his door quietly.

I asked, "What are you guys issued for rifles and side arms?"

"For our Parks and Recreation areas, we are issued a 12-gauge shotgun, with one-ounce slugs and double-aught buck loads, mainly used for bear problems. Our sidearm is a .357 Magnum revolver."

I had no doubt of Stewart's ability to use either weapon, as the RCMP requires shooting hours every month, to stay qualified. A shotgun shooting slugs is great for close quarters, from 80 to 100 yards, maximum. Its effectiveness is reduced beyond that distance, as the slug loses velocity and drops like the arc of a rainbow. In this terrain, the shotgun would work fine, since in the thick brush and dense tree cover, a shooter wouldn't usually get a clear shot beyond its effective, lethal distance anyway.

I asked Stewart for his opinion. "How far is that 12-gauge good for with your one-ounce slugs? Have you tested it at any distance?"

"I terminated a troublesome grizzly last summer at Cameron Lake with two shots. The distance was just shy of one hundred yards and the second shot sent him to bear heaven. But I think on a human, it would do collateral damage a bit farther."

"Yeah, it would be scary being shot at a hundred yards with a one-ounce pumpkin ball crashing near you. Being shot at with double-aught buckshot, those nine-thirty-eight caliber balls would certainly put the fear of God in you at any range."

While Stewart finished securing his weapons and pack, I ate another roll from the bag Mrs. Higgs sent with us. I handed the bag to Stewart, who grabbed one and put the remainder in the truck.

We began our approach up a small ridge toward the parking area, staying off the roadway. From the top of the ridge, we'd be able to see the end of the road.

From the ridge top, we saw their stock trucks parked below. There were three stock trucks, with side racks to load horses and gear into. Three pickup trucks were hitched up to horse trailers. They were all parked near the horse-loading ramp. If a passerby saw this group of vehicles, they would only assume there was a horse party heading down into the Belly River Valley for a camping and fishing trip. It all looked quite innocent, as this is a fairly common sight, especially in the summer months.

From the ridge, I detailed to Eric the rest of the terrain we would be working in, and the location of the trail that exited near the parking area. We kept our focus on the vehicles to see if there were any life forms, knowing someone likely stayed there as a precaution, or was posted there after yesterday's shootings. We needed to close the gap toward the trucks soon, as the riders we scoped earlier would be arriving within the next hour. There was no indication that anyone was around or in the parking area, but we were not discounting the chance that someone could be somewhere in the vicinity.

We needed to move closer, staying in cover, while we closed the gap to the vehicles. Reaching the bottom of a shallow ravine, we angled toward the parking area, with anticipation that someone was there. When we were well within two hundred yards, Stewart went to the left and I edged in from the opposite direction. This put us on opposite sides of the trucks. With my rifle ready in hand, I kept my pace slow, deliberate and cautious. I was hoping there would be no more shooting, especially before the pack string showed up. The sound of shots would warn the others and the result could be really ugly for our situation. I am sure Stewart had similar thoughts.

Stewart was nearby, perched on top a rocky knob above the trucks on the opposite side from me. I crouched down and moved toward the closest truck, hoping Stewart would be able to cover me from his roost.

Crouching under the stock truck by the dual rear wheels, I listened and watched for any clue, a sound or anything that might indicate where a guard could be. I finally heard what sounded like the squeak of a truck chassis, and figured someone was in the back of one of the trucks. I looked at the rear end of each stock truck and noticed hay strewn below the trailer hitch of one of the flatbeds. The loose hay was on the ground beneath it, and obviously, the hitch was there from being tracked outside by many exits. I lurked closer to the truck where I suspected someone was inside. This particular truck had canvas-tarped stock racks on its sides and over the top of the bed, forming a tent. As I got closer, I could hear a raspy noise coming from inside, with a slow rhythmic pattern. It was obvious that someone was sleeping in the back, and snoring. Sleeping on top of the hay bales made for a comfortable bunk, but was there more than one person inside? Tiptoeing slowly, careful to not to step on anything that might make noise, I edged alongside the truck toward the rear of the bed. I noticed a tire iron lying on the ground by the back tires. I grabbed it with my free hand.

The back of the truck bed also had a canvas tarp draped over its top where they were tied off at the bed, or on the stakes of the truck. The tarped-over stock racks made a cozy, dark, tent-like structure inside its canvassed walls. With the addition of hay bales, this made a dry place to bunk, out of the weather. I was hoping the guy inside was napping really hard. I prayed he was the only person there.

In back, the opening of the tarp was split in the middle, with the side farthest from me tied open for entry and exit, and for a bit of light to enter. The frame for the trailer hitch below the bed created a step to climb in and out. I wondered, "How am I going to be able to look inside without being seen?" The heavy, raspy breathing continued its regular pattern, so I knew at least one guy was asleep. But, was there another inside? I had to know. I couldn't just open the flap and look in. I was in a hurry, as the pack string might show up at any time. Eric and I had to quickly lessen the odds and control this situation, before the others arrived.

A slight breeze kicked up occasionally, lightly ruffling the canvas opening. I reached up and grabbed the rope that held the flap door open. During the next breeze ruffle, I pulled the slipknot loose and the opening closed. I waited, poised for someone inside to exit and tie the flap open. I heard movement inside while the snoring continued. I knew there was at least one other person inside. The flap opened outward and a cowboy boot extended out and down to the first rung on the trailer hitch. As the second foot came down to the second rung, I struck a downward, hard blow at the ankle on the bridge of the foot, with the tire iron. The man buckled, falling to the ground, grabbing for his foot and screaming as he fell. I smacked him once more across the upper back below the neck, as he landed headfirst on the hard-packed ground. It was a five-foot fall from the bed to the dirt. He lay motionless, as the pain, and his head-plant on the ground, must have knocked him cold. His scream aroused movement inside, as the snores stopped. The flap flew open again. I had already moved around to the side of the truck, out of sight. A raspy voice said,

"Billy? Bill? Bill? What the hell! Hey, Bill, you hear me? You alright?" Then there was silence for a moment. A big boot stepped down to the first rung, just as Bill had done moments before. I waited for this man to get both feet on the ground and said from behind him, "Don't move, you're under arrest," as I placed the barrel muzzle in his back. "Now, lay face down, your belly in the dirt, next to your buddy, Bill." As I pushed the rifle barrel against his back with a little more force, I said, "Move it now, and no cute stuff. I am not alone."

The man went down to his knees, and then to push-up position, and lowered his gut to the dirt. Placing my knee on his back, I pulled his hands behind his back, placed flex-cuffs on his wrists and gagged him with his own bandana. I did the same to the unconscious Bill, lying next to him.

Stewart climbed down off his little rocky knoll, just as I was finishing up with Bill. He said, "How did you know there were two of them?"

"I didn't. I was only expecting one," I said, as Stewart pointed at Bill with his shotgun barrel.

"I saw this guy fall hard. Ya think he broke his neck?" he said, concerned.

"I don't think it's broken. I hope not anyway, he's still breathing, he might have a slight concussion," I said calmly.

"Those guys leading the pack string this way should be arriving real soon. Let's get set up for their welcoming, and check out the trail-head for places to safely position ourselves."

"Well, let's go kid, I'll cover you," Stewart said in a mocked-up John Wayne voice.

I just shook my head and grinned. "Over here," I pointed, while moving toward the trail that headed into the Belly River Valley from Lee Ridge.

S tewart and I quickly hoofed it down the trail to the first switchback, where he positioned himself in the brush on the uphill side of the trail. This section of trail had been laid with corduroy planking. I went back up the trail about 50 feet to where the planking joined back with the dirt trail. Corduroy is planking which is spiked to log stringers that are suspended on the tops of piers, wherever continual muddy areas exist on trails. Off both sides of the corduroy decking, and on the ground below, is a sloppy, muddy mess. This forces hikers and horses to walk directly on the corduroy planking. The corduroy walkway is only wide enough for single file horse travel, and measures six feet in width. A pack string must travel slowly over this kind of trail section, in single file. If a horse were to spook and step off the plank walkway, the result would be instant panic for the animal, as its hooves and legs would quickly sink into the sloppy, quicksand-like mud. If the remaining pack-string were dragged in after that horse, this would become a packer's nightmare. Horse packers call this fiasco a "wreck," as it's an awful situation to straighten out. This is a bad dream for any horse packer.

I planted myself on the uphill side of the wooden trail. "I'll stop the led rider just before the horse is about to step from the last few planks back onto the dirt trail," I thought. That way, Stewart will be uphill and perpendicular to the last rider, and the horses will be stopped on the corduroy. From his position, he can cover me and hold the second rider at bay. With both of us set up on the uphill side of the trail, the poachers will be directly in front of us, like a shooting gallery. This arrangement will make it possible for me to talk to the first poacher without the last man being able to hear the conversation. Stewart can keep the last man at gunpoint, holding him there with ease. He'll be trapped, having pack animals in front and behind, with the sloppy mud below each side of the planking. I squatted down behind a blown-down fir tree, about 20 feet on the uphill side of the trail. This put me a little higher in elevation than the other riders. Both Stewart and I will have the afternoon sun against our backs, shining in the poachers' eyes. We will have full advantage of the situation in this position. If there were gunplay, they would be extremely disadvantaged, being out in the open with no place to go except into the mud. I looked along the trail to Stewart, who was motioning down the switchback, saying softly, "They are down one switchback from us, hear them?"

I nodded yes. "The next switchback turn they make will bring them right back toward you. It's a short section of trail, get set," I said with enough voice for him to hear.

The sounds of the horses' hooves were closing in, and Stewart had a visual on them. I could see movement through the trees, and was barely able make out the first rider. He was the same character that shot at me yesterday morning, when this whole thing exploded into a manhunt.

The first rider made the turn onto the last switchback. They were heading onto our section of corduroy, where Stewart and I were in ambush. Each poacher was leading two pack animals, loaded down with elk meat and head capes. Each pack animal had an eight- or seven-point elk rack straddling the top of the Decker packsaddles. Both felons rode with their reins in hand above the saddle horn, while their other hands rested on their thighs. The horses began their advance onto the corduroy in follow-the-leader single file. The boardwalk thundered with the drumming hoofbeats against it.

When the led villain was near the end of the corduroy, I stood up with my rifle aimed at his head. "Stop, and freeze," I ordered. He appeared shocked and startled, looking to where he had heard the voice. He saw the barrel of the carbine aimed at his face. A shot at that range would be difficult to miss, and he knew it. He reined his horse to a stop. "Just sit there and don't move, keep your hands in the open where I can see them," I commanded.

I could hear Stewart's distant voice surprising the second rider and demanding that he and his pack animals halt.

I kept my rifle aimed, while moving closer. I ordered him, "Let down your led rope slowly and keep both hands in sight. You had your chance at me yesterday morning, and missed. Today, at this range, I can't miss," I said calmly. His hand let go of the rope as it rolled off his thigh to the planking.

"Now raise your hands higher, slowly, and keep them above your shoulders." I moved toward him with the rifle still pointed at him. I grabbed his reins at the bit and pulled the remainder of the latigo straps from the saddle, to the trail. Reaching toward the saddle, I slid his rifle forward, out of the scabbard, and removed the clip from the magazine. I threw the rifle downhill, into the mud a few feet beyond the planking.

I could hear Eric Stewart's voice directing instructions to his prisoner, although I could not make out his words. His horseman was dismounting slowly, while Stewart kept his shotgun steadily focused.

"All right now, get off that horse slowly," I ordered, "and let's move real slow, like cold honey in the wintertime. The hammer on this carbine is cocked." My prisoner looked calm and asked, "Can I lower a hand to dismount, for balance?"

I told him "Yes, but again, keep your hands in sight and do it slowly." I felt this man was acting excessively calm and poised under the circumstances. So, I watched his movements carefully.

His left hand lowered slowly to the saddle horn as his right hand dropped toward the swell of the saddle. His right leg swung back over the rump of the horse. That's when I saw his pistol under his coattails.

As his right hand moved back toward the rear of the saddle, instead of grabbing for the cantle, he slipped it underneath his coat to the revolver. I stepped back, jerking the reins forward, hard; the horse lunged. As the rider had his left foot in the stirrup, he lost his balance. As he fell backward, he reached, with his pistol in hand, to break his fall. His left hand still gripped the saddle horn as he attempted to regain control. Using my rifle, I swung and slammed the barrel down on the saddle horn, crunching his knuckles between the barrel and the horn. He let out a grunt as he fell to the corduroy decking. I lunged forward, swinging the carbine by the pistol grip of the stock, like a hatchet, laying the barrel across the back of the fallen man's head. His body relaxed and lay still on the edge of the corduroy, with his legs hanging over the planks and his boots in the mud. I picked up his pistol and tucked it behind my belt.

It had all happened so quickly, I just stood, stunned, for a moment. I felt my knees shaking; my heart was pounding and I was breathing heavily from the brief, almost deadly, skirmish. This could have ended the other way around, with me lying at his feet, shot and dying, or already dead. I was lucky to see his pistol when I did. I should have checked him for more weapons. This could have been my final trail.

"Hey Stewart, I'll be there in a minute, to frisk that guy, but I want to get the cuffs on this clown while he's not moving. Check your guy for a pistol, and knife, too."

He replied, "We are not going anywhere. No problem here and no need to hurry."

I placed flex-cuffs on his wrists and pulled him back up on the corduroy deck. Then I frisked him good. I pulled the sheath knife from his belt, which had dried blood and fat on it, from field-dressing an animal. I kept it for evidence. I went through his pockets and found the keys to some trucks in the parking area. There were two sets of them. I led his horse and pack animals off the corduroy and hitched them to a tree trunk. I then went to where Stewart still had his man at gunpoint.

Stewart looked up, and said, "This guy has been real cooperative."

"Yeah, that character back there and I already met yesterday, briefly." Eric Stewart had his shotgun focused at the back of his prisoner, who still had his hands held high. The captive turned his head slowly in my direction, and I saw a familiar face.

His name was Tommy Feather, a gas station and storeowner in the St. Mary area, outside the east entrance to the park. Tommy and I had never formally met, but it was common knowledge on the east side of the divide that Feather's Trading Post had the cheapest gas and the coldest beer north of Browning. I filled up my rig there, many times before heading back over the Going-to-the-Sun Road on my way home for my days off. It appeared Tommy did a booming tourist business in the summer months. His trading post was like a convenience store and curio shop, which sold local arts and crafts. The items he sold varied from hand-forged tomahawks and handmade leather moccasins to native jewelry, custom-made knives, beadwork, wildlife paintings, tee shirts and more. In July and August, the store was open from 6 a.m. to midnight. His shop was an eye-catching place, with its rustic, rough-sawn wood and flat storefront, giving it an old-time trading-post flair, or general store appearance. On the porch were two wooden Indians, for an old-fashioned, aesthetic atmosphere.

"Tommy, what's the matter? The tourist season not making you enough money these days?" I said to let him know that I knew who he was.

"Keep your act clean now, Tommy, and you'll be able to work your trading post again, sooner than later."

"I'll cooperate and won't give you no funny stuff, honest. I got talked into this mess, with some of the rest of these guys. Ned up there, the guy on the ground, and his brother, said it was real easy and fun, exciting and profitable, and that nothing could go wrong. It was a stupid decision, and the other new guys that came along also feel the same. This was just a plain, dumb move. For a few of us, this was our first time doing this hunt. A couple of the others had been hunting here for three years without a glitch, until yesterday morning."

"Had you all been a day later, I'd already have left the Belly River Ranger Station, and no one would have been the wiser," I told him. "Now get down on your belly, flat on the ground with your hands behind your back."

Tommy moved slowly to the ground and did as instructed. While I was putting on the wrist cuffs, Tommy asked, "Are you the same ranger that was in there yesterday?"

"Yep, that was me. Now get up." I helped him to his feet by pulling on his jacket shoulders to get him to stand.

"How'd you get here so fast? We had people at trail exits, and searchers were combing all over that valley for you." He motioned with a nod of his head toward the man I had had the encounter with and said, "Ned sent his brother, Nat, over Stoney Indian Pass to check Goat Haunt Station to see if you had made it that far, by chance."

"I know," I said. "We met this morning."

"Damn!" He said in a surprised voice.

"Stew, let's tie up old Ned a little better, before he comes to."

"Yep, he might go nuts when he finds out his brother is dead. Well I have a way of tying up monsters like this, so they don't struggle much, and it keeps them more manageable."

"Tommy, you have a seat on that there corduroy's edge and relax a moment, and stay put," I told him. I grabbed the led rope to Tommy's horse and walked them both up to the other horses. Then, I tied his horse's reins to the pigging string of the last packhorse in Ned's string.

"Tommy, come on up here. I want you in front of me," as I pointed up the trail with my carbine still in hand.

He started up the trail past the horses, with me trailing right behind. He spoke to me in passing, "Sir don't worry, and I won't try anything. Maybe good behavior will help me out later in court."

Stewart had Ned really tied up. Stewart had taken one of the horse's reins, tied it around Ned's neck with a slipknot and then ran it down his back to his cuffed hands, where it was tied directly to the cuffs. If Ned struggled and moved his hands, the reins would tighten around his neck and slow, or stop his breathing, until he quit struggling.

"You like his new necktie?" Stewart asked.

"Heck, yeah, I like it a lot" I replied.

"This just flat works; I use it all the time. In Canada we generally do this to all unruly persons, but our wrist cuffs already have a neck chain attached to them, so it's quicker to apply."

"Is Ned showing any signs of life, yet?" I asked.

"Yeah, he moves and kind of softly groans once in awhile. He has quite a big mouse on the back of his head. Do you think your rifle barrel is bent from that blow, and is still accurate?" Stewart's grin was devilish, at this comment. "He'll come to in a little while. Then we can get on back to the trucks. He's too big to try to drag or carry."

"Tommy, I want the truth. When is the rest of your party supposed to be coming up the trail? So, what is the actual plan for the rest of today? If you cooperate, it might help in court, although I can't guarantee it. I'll put in a good word for you." I was hoping to get some reliable information. Tommy told us, "The rest of us are all supposed to be here about 4 o'clock...what time is it now?"

"It's almost 3 o'clock," Stewart answered impatiently.

"We are supposed to make sure everybody is here no later than 6 o'clock today." Tommy explained.

"How many more gunmen are still down there?"

"Ten, plus one is being packed out and maybe one more, if they found Ned's brother, Nat."

"Were you all planning to leave this evening? Or spending the night?" I needed to know.

"No. We were all going to get our stories straight about what happened. Then a couple guys were going to go to various possible exit sites for tonight and tomorrow and wait till you showed up. Nat was supposed to go to Goat Haunt and wait in ambush for you, if you went there. The rest of us were supposed to leave with some stock, all the meat, capes and racks," Tommy said.

"What were Ned's plans, once you both got back here to the trucks?"

"The two guys here were supposed to be waiting to help get us unsaddled and unpacked. Then we'd load up the trucks and leave. The four of us were going to head for home with two of the trucks, and stash the elk somewhere safe where it would not be found. That was the plan."

Ned was starting to gain more life by the minute.

"Dang, Stewart, I wish I had my radio. I could probably contact St. Mary Ranger Station directly from here. With four of these bad guys here, and more coming, it would be nice to have some backup, quickly."

"Let's take everything we've got here, leave for St. Mary Ranger Station, and inform the rangers of all the details. Then they can come out and nab the rest of these guys, later today or tomorrow." Stewart said.

I grabbed the canteen from Ned's saddle, and poured some of the cold water on his head and face. Ned's eyes opened and he looked up at the three of us standing over him. He was getting his bearings, and remembering what happened, and why his head and knuckles were hurting.

I told Ned. "Don't try and struggle, as this Mountie tied you up good. You will only make yourself more uncomfortable. Now, help us help you to your feet."

Stewart and I each grabbed one of the shoulders of his heavy winter coat and hoisted him to his feet. He was wobbling out of balance at first, but we held him to give him time to steady himself. Then we all trekked up the trail together, with Ned and Tommy leading, and Eric and I following right behind. I led the horses and pack animals while Stewart guarded the prisoners.

13

A few minutes later, we arrived at the trailhead working our way toward the trucks. I could see Tommy turn and say something to Stewart, but I was trailing too far behind with the noisy pack string to hear the words.

Then I saw Stewart motion for Tommy to approach me. I had no clue what was going on, but soon found out when Tommy explained, "Your radio is in Ned's saddle bag. Don't let on that I told you. Ned might be very unpredictable if he found out I told you. There is no telling what he might do to me or my family later." I told Tommy, "Thanks, I'll keep it secret." I was starting to feel a bit more trusting toward Tommy.

As Tommy and I walked together, he began to explain his story. "This whole hunting trip was so enticing and exciting. However, once we started into Belly River, I wished I'd never gotten involved. It was all wrong in my mind, but it was too late to turn back. I was committed, and felt I couldn't just leave and lose face with the rest of the guys. I have a good business with my trading post. I make a good living for my family. I guess I felt the need for a little excitement and some fellowship with the guys. The first time I decided to go along, we were caught, and two of my friends are dead. I feel like such a fool for being part of this outlaw activity. I made a selfish and stupid decision."

"It will all work out, Tommy. And thanks for the tip on the radio."

When we arrived at the trucks, I said, "Ned, those keys I took from you, do they fit these trucks?"

In his bitterness, he said, "You figure it out, Mr. Pine Pig."

Tommy was staring at me and then motioned with his eyes to the stock truck to our left. "Gee, Ned, I think I'll try this one that says Ford on the keys. They usually seem to start Fords." I was needling Ned and I was totally enjoying it. It was not very professional of me, I know, "But, what the heck," I thought. After what I had been through for the last two days, it felt good to shoot a few bullets of sarcasm at the ringleader. I turned and went to the truck that Tommy had motioned to. I jumped in and the first key I tried fired up the engine. I turned the ignition off again, leaving the keys.

"Stewart, what do you say we tie these guys up in the back of the truck with the evidence, secure them to the stake sides, and haul them into St. Mary?"

"Let's get a move on, before the rest of the bandits show up and we have a confrontation, and can't leave quickly, or at all," Stewart replied. So, we boosted Tommy and Ned into the back of the flatbed. Stewart began tying them to the stakes while I began stripping the packs from the horses. Pulling the saddle off Ned's horse, I opened the saddlebags and found my park handset radio. Transmitting from here would be a direct shot to St. Mary Ranger Station, without having to transmit through a repeater that likely still wasn't repaired.

"Yo, Stewart, I've found my radio in the saddle bags on Ned's horse." I could hear Ned cussing softly in the back of the truck.

"Get on the air," he yelled from the truck, where he was tying up our prisoners.

I switched on the radio. The batteries were still charged. I clicked the transmit button and said, "745, this is 225 Alpha. 745, this is 225 Alpha, 10-18," meaning "urgent."

"This is 745. Go ahead," the radio immediately squawked back. It was Russ Kiser, the sub-district ranger for the Saint Mary district of the park. He was head honcho, and one heck of a good man.

"I've arrested four poachers with evidence. 10-20 is the old Chief Mountain Oil Road Trailhead parking area. There are nine more poachers riding out of the Belly River Valley with an E.T.A. of one-and-a-half hours, or less. Need assistance, now. There has been some shooting and two subjects are dead. Working with me is a Waterton Townsite Canadian Mountie, Eric Stewart. We are leaving the trail-head within five minutes with the four prisoners, four Decker pack saddles loaded with elk meat, bull-elk capes, elk antlers and other evidence."

"We will meet up with you somewhere along the highway. I'll be in a blue, Ford flatbed stock truck with the staked sides, tarped. A green RCMP pickup will be following me."

"Ten-four, 745 copy."

"225 Alpha out," I signed off and turned off the radio. During the next ten minutes, there would be lot of radio chatter while they were getting things organized to meet us. I didn't want to hear the noise, and I didn't want the additional, arriving riders to be alerted by the radio chatter as they were entering into the parking area. I yelled to Stewart, "I'll keep working on getting the horses unpacked and loaded, and then we'll get the hell out of Dodge, because Hell might be coming to supper early."

I continued removing the gear from the horses and piling it onto the bed of the truck. Stewart went to where we left the other two prisoners. Bill was conscious. Stewart led them to the back of the truck, one at a time, lashing them to the side stakes.

Ned yelled, "Hey Ranger, you said two of us were dead. I only know of one. Where's the other one? Or are you just trying to make yourself look good to your boss?"

"Sorry, Ned, but I shot two men to save my life," I replied.

"You're lying. There is no way you are good enough to get two of these boys. You're not that smart or sharp," he poked, with a mean, sarcastic voice.

"I might not be, but I was definitely luckier than those two were."

I kept busy removing the packs and gave him the silent treatment. However, Ned wouldn't let up.

"Where was it that you shot the second one, Mr. Hero Pine Pig?"

"I shot him in the chest," I said, matter-of-factly. That got Ned fired up. He was losing his cool.

"You friggin' jerk! Where was he shot? What location?" Ned yelled violently.

I didn't answer, and just kept working on the packs as fast as I could. We needed to get out of there. With big-mouthed Ned yelling, any of the others coming up the trail could hear him, and would be warned something was wrong.

I could hear Tommy saying something in a low voice to Ned. Then, Ned exploded vocally, calling me every name in his nasty little book of words, with a few in a different language mixed in. I figured Tommy must have told him that his brother was dead. I said to Stewart, "If Ned doesn't shut up, put a gag on him." Ned got quiet, moments later.

Stewart left the truck bed, with the two other captives tied up and said to me, "Are you learning any new cussing vocabulary from Ned, Mister Pine Pig?"

Again, Ned was hurling threats at me saying, "I'll get you for this, I swear I will. Someday, I'll even the score with you, Ranger Pig. My brother was too good with a gun, and good in the woods; he was one of the best hunters and best shots around. There is no way you could have got the drop on him. No cheap Federal Pig like you could ever get one over on him," Ned screamed.

"Stewart, I am just about done with these packs, and Ned's making enough noise to warn the entire territory. Let's get a move on, quickly. Jump in the back with the prisoners, and I'll drive down to your truck. Then, you follow me to St. Mary,"

Stewart replied, "Once we are on the highway, if I blink my headlights on and off, pull over, as there might be trouble in the back of the truck."

"Good plan, thanks," I told him. I hoisted the last of the packs up to Stewart, as he had just finished his task in the bed. "That's it. Let's go," I said, stepping toward the cab of the truck.

"Hey, wait a minute. Just in case, cover me. I am going to pull the coil wires off these trucks so we can't be followed, and they can't leave." Stewart said.

"Go for it! I'll start this rig so we are ready to go. I'll cover you." Stewart jumped out of the back of the truck and ran over to the nearest truck, popped the hood open, and jerked the wire out. Then he closed the hood, and moved on from truck to truck, with youthful quickness. I kept an eye on the trailhead, in case anyone showed up. Stewart had three pickups left to do, on the opposite side of the parking area, when a rider and pack string crested the rise from the trailhead. Stewart had just popped the hood up and was hidden behind it, when the rider appeared. My truck was idling. I stood on the step of the cab, with the truck's rear end facing the trailhead. Hearing the idling truck, the rider looked. I was completely out of his sight, except for the top of my head peeking over the tarped headache rack. I was positioned to shoot from the step of the cab, using the top of the stake rails as a steady rest for the rifle. Stewart slammed the hood. The rider turned and looked Stewart's way, when he heard the hood slam shut. Eric had seen him first, and ducked out of sight.

I raised and aimed my rifle at the rider, who was less than a hundred yards from me. If he even looked like he was going to draw a rifle and fire, I'd have to shoot him. It would be a tough shot at that distance, with open sights and the truck vibrating from the idling engine. I couldn't keep the rifle perfectly steady. The horse's head was covering the largest part of the rider's body, also.

"Larry, he's behind the green Dodge," Ned yelled from where he watched, inside the back of the truck. "Shoot him," he screeched.

I steadied the rifle on the top horizontal slat of the stakes, and held the sights on the rider. Out of the corner of my eye, I saw Stewart move to the next nearest truck. Then Eric had about forty yards of exposure between himself and my truck.

The rider drew his rifle from the scabbard as he watched for movement for a target. I shot, low into the dirt just in front of the horse, which made the animal crow-hop sideways, and turn a bit. Then I could get a sight on the man's torso, a much easier shot. I didn't want to kill him; I had done enough of that already. I just wanted to injure him enough to keep him from shooting at, and hitting, Stewart. Eric sprinted for the truck. As the rider raised his rifle to shoot, I squeezed the trigger of my cocked rifle. The rider jerked and almost fell from his mount, but hung onto the saddle horn to stay mounted, and dropped his rifle to the ground in the process.

Stewart jumped to the step on the passenger side of the cab, slamming his hand against the cab roof repeatedly while yelling, "Go, Go, Go!" I sprang into the seat behind the wheel, and we were hauling down the road toward Stewart's vehicle. As I drove, Stewart climbed back along the rails of the stock truck rack and entered the back of the flatbed with the prisoners. I pulled up and stopped near his truck's hiding place. Jumping out of the back, he yelled, as he was sprinting toward his truck, "Go on, I'll catch up with you. Get moving!"

I was bouncing down the dirt road. I wished Stewart had had the chance to get the coil wires from the last two pickups and put them out of service. I had enough challenges and excitement in the past two days, and didn't want any additional, so-called "action." I especially didn't want a highway chase scene. I only wanted St. Mary law enforcement rangers, and every other available ranger from the east side of the park, to be heading our way to relieve us of the mess we left behind.

When I hit the pavement, Stewart caught up to me and was flashing his headlights, so I pulled onto the shoulder of the road. He climbed out of his truck, ran up to me, jumped up on the cab step and asked, "What's the big hurry?"

I told him I was concerned about the last two trucks, which he did not incapacitate.

"Oh, yes I did. I crawled underneath, out of sight, and cut the lower radiator hoses. They won't be going far in those vehicles." He had a smirk on his face.

"You don't miss a trick, do you? Thanks, that gives me a lot of stress relief. I was really concerned when that last poacher showed up, that they would try and chase us down, to help their buddies."

Stewart replied, "So was I. Good shooting. Thanks for the cover fire."

I grinned, saying nonchalantly, "See? I must not have bent the barrel over Ned's head, or you'd have been shot."

Stewart just shook his head with a chuckle.

"Thanks to Ned's big mouth, you were getting all the attention. He didn't realize I was even there, till my first shot. That moved his horse, so I could get a better pop at him. That shot totally confused him," I said excitedly. "I don't think the followup shot hit him in any vitals. I think the bullet struck him high in the shoulder."

"Yeah, that was lucky." Stewart said with a sigh. "I already thanked Ned in the back of the truck, for aiding in the confusion, when his pal, Larry, showed up."

"I'll bet Ned really appreciated the note of gratitude," I laughed.

14

———

"Let's take these nimrods on in. We should meet up with the rangers from St. Mary in a few minutes, I am thinking. Stewart, how about a hand on the paperwork when we get there?" I said hopefully.

"No problem. I'll need something to do to calm me down before I hit the hay tonight; anyway, with all this excitement, it rather got me all fired-up. It might be hard to get to sleep," He explained.

I told him, "Thanks, let's get this dog-and-pony-show out of here, before something else happens."

He ran back to his truck and we started down the deserted highway again. My thoughts raced through my head about all I had been through during the past two days, and a wave of exhaustion washed over me. I was only a seasonal ranger, and was blessed to still be alive. Permanent rangers train and prepare all year long, in case they get involved with some kind of felonious activity. My training consisted of a week and a half of daily classes and some fieldwork, at the beginning of each summer. It included a day at the shooting range, to qualify trainees for bear management. The magnitude of this poaching incident was entirely unexpected, and was an unheard-of surprise for a seasonal, or even a permanent worker to be involved in. I knew that permanents also would have been caught off-guard under these same circumstances. The timing of this incident just happened to occur on my watch, and I was instantly entangled in it. This was a unique series of events that I was tangled in. I observed the scene of the crime; I was detected, and then shot at. At that point, the game was on. It all happened so quickly that, in a twinkle, I was running for my life.

The November sun was sinking low in the big Montana sky behind me, throwing shadows of the mountain silhouettes eastward; in the direction I was driving. Rumbling down the seasonally used road, I became aware again of my shoulder, with its continual aching. It was the first time since we had left Waterton Townsite that I had given it much thought. I thought to myself, "When I get to St. Mary, I'll have the EMT take a look at it for any infection, clean it up and redress it with fresh dressings."

On the flats up ahead, where the plains meet the Rocky Mountains a few miles down the road, I detected a small convoy of vehicles heading toward us with their headlights on. I turned on my headlights, to show my presence and location. I pulled off the pavement at the first large turnout I came to, with Stewart following right behind me.

Climbing out of the cab of the truck, I felt the blast of crisp, cold air of the late autumn afternoon on my hands and unshaved face. Stewart moseyed up next to me, as we waited for the patrol to arrive.

A total of 14 rangers showed up in six vehicles; some were in Park Service crew cabs with others in patrol cars. All vehicles were decaled with green, "Law Enforcement" decals on the white vehicles' sides, and equipped with light bars on top of the cabs. Russ was in the led rig. He was out of his vehicle first, with everyone else piling out of his or her rigs, following right behind him.

"Hey, are you OK, Big Guy?" Russ asked.

"Yeah, I am doing well. A bit fatigued and drained, but it has been an unusually treacherous two days." As everyone grouped around us, I introduced Eric Stewart. Then Eric and I explained the situation they'd find up the old Oil Well Road at the trailhead. After a few minutes of discussion and planning, they were back in their rigs and on their way to gather and apprehend, hopefully without incident, the remaining bottom-feeding desperados.

Russ mentioned to me that two FBI agents were on their way from Cut Bank, and should be at St. Mary Ranger Station when Stewart and I arrived.

Both of us returned to our vehicles. I started driving out of the pullout. I stopped immediately and backed up from where I had just left. I thought I'd better check the handcuffs and ropes of our prisoners once more. Stewart pulled forward and parked in front of my truck and got out. I said to him loudly, "I probably should check on the guys in back again."

He replied, "You want an extra hand?"

I told him, 'I think I got it, thanks."

"Ok, I'll wait here," Stewart said, loud enough to be heard in the evening breeze. I climbed up into the bed and checked Tommy's wrists first. He was still fastened securely, although I didn't expect much trouble from him.

"Any of you boys need a saddle blanket thrown over you to break the chill?" I asked.

Ned said casually, "Yeah, I need one. Throw one of those thicker blankets over my legs, would you?"

I yanked a blanket out from underneath a saddle, stepped over to Ned and bent down to lay it across his lower body.

With the quickness of a striking snake, Ned's right fist came up from behind his back and connected on my left cheek. I had already been a little off balance, when he made full contact with my face. The sucker smack stunned me as I was slowly tipping backward, dazed and surprised by the sudden assault. I forced myself to roll back hard, coming up on my feet with my back bouncing against the sides of the stock rack. Ned was springing toward me off his haunches, to tackle and take me down to the deck of the truck bed. My right knee came up hard and caught him square in the nose, as he was trying to grab on to my lower body; I could feel the cartilage breaking against my thigh. The rest of his forward thrust slammed me back into the stakes again, as his arms wrapped around my waist. Again, I bounced back hard, into the stock racks, against my back. I twisted to shake him off, and threw my right arm deep into his right armpit that was wrapped around my lower back. I stood up hard, and jerked my body to the left to loosen his squeeze, enough that I could place my forearm deeper, with a whizzer counter on him. With a whizzer, his arm was wrapped around my lower back and was locked in place, with my elbow joint directly in his armpit. I had control of his upper body and head. I had wrestled a bit in college and coached high school wrestling, and I liked this move. I heaved my whizzer arm straight upward, lifting hard, which brought Ned's shoulder upward, and his head followed. With my left arm and balled up fist, I telegraphed a sweeping, hard punch upward into his face, driving Ned upward as my whizzer arm forced him over, backward. My right foot quickly stepped behind his boots, making him trip, and fall backward. I brought him down to the bed for the takedown, with my knee landing painfully in his gut. Ned's face was smeared with blood from his smashed nose. I have always had a bad temper when pushed too far. I had lost all control. I dropped down into a Saturday Night Ride position and proceeded to slam my right fist into his face, over and over again. I had the advantage, as I outweighed Ned by at least 40 pounds and was taller by eight inches. Suddenly, the back of my collar was being tugged on, hard. I commenced to turn and grab for whoever was behind me. I was in frenzy. Then I heard Stewart's panicked voice yell, "Stop, you're going to kill him. Lay off, Man," as he attempted to pull me off Ned.

I stopped my fury, feeling exhausted, with my heart pounding. I was a little lightheaded, like being woken from a bad dream. I sat there on Ned for a few moments, breathing heavily. Ned was unconscious and there was no fight left in him. He was lying still, and behaving as he should. After a few moments, I had gathered my composure. Stewart helped me stand up. I could barely stand, as my legs were shaking from the adrenalin rush that had just played out in this skirmish. Ned lay there motionless. It was a beautiful sight. He would no longer be any trouble on this trip. He was down for the count, and maybe longer. This wicked man shot at me, and then later tried to pull his pistol and shoot me. He had just tried to take control of the situation once more. I was actually feeling good about the thrashing I had just given him.

Stewart giggled and said, "Ol' Ned's head sure got quite a workout today, between your banging the rifle on the back of it and playing punching bag with his face. He's had quite an afternoon. He'll have a headache later, eh?" I didn't answer. My fist hurt and began to swell. My wounded left shoulder was hurting, too. It was weeping again, running down my chest and back. Stewart knelt down next to Ned, rolled him over and put his last pair of steel handcuffs on him. Eric mentioned, "I had always heard those flex-cuffs could be broken, or gnawed away against something until they broke. It looks like Ned used the upright steel stake edge to grind his way through them. When Ned's hands were free, he went to work untying the choke rope while pretending he was still tied up. He was waiting for a chance, either to get away or to get hold of the situation by eliminating one or both of us."

"Ned's no quitter, I'll give him that. He moves like a cat, and hits hard too!" I said this as I felt the mouse on my cheekbone. "I am glad I smashed his other hand on the saddle horn now, otherwise I might have been hit with that one, too."

"I've checked the other three prisoners and they are all secure. Plus, I don't think they will want to give you any trouble, after seeing the whipping you just gave to their ring leader," Stewart said with a chuckle, and as a warning to the others listening. "Isn't that right, fellas?" he asked, looking at them. They all seemed congenial and nodded in reply. "Dang, I wish I was big like you," Stewart said, grinning. Then I asked, "Why? It's just more body area, and places for you to have hurting."

I began feeling more like myself again and said, "Let's go. I want this day to be left behind me as quickly as possible. I've had enough. This cop-and-killer stuff is hard on a guy's body and nerves," as I looked at my aching hand that was swelling from the abuse I had just given it on Ned's face.

"Let's get this circus back on the road. Besides, I am hungry," Stewart said.

"Yep, I am too," I chimed in.

15

We jumped down from the back of the truck, got back into our cabs, and continued on toward St. Mary. On the road, I could see in the large, rearview door mirror that the sun was looking for a place to camp for its evening nap.

We turned into the ranger station parking area as the alpenglow was beginning to show off its tangerine, sunburnt radiance across the St. Mary Valley. A few small, puffy, pinkish clouds were suspended low in the autumn sky.

The Federal Bureau of Investigation car was parked in front of the sub-district office, so I parked the stock truck beside it. Stewart did the same. As I stepped out of the cab, two FBI agents exited the office door and walked down the pathway to greet us with introductions.

"Hi, I am Jim Jensen and this is Thom Barker. We are agents out of Cut Bank, to back you up on this case before it goes to court."

"Howdy, I heard you would be here. This is Eric Stewart, RCMP, who helped make these arrests possible." We all shook hands. Out of habit, I used my handshaking hand that was injured. That was a bad mistake. It hurt worse from the handshaking. "Dumb move," I thought to myself.

"We have four prisoners in the back of this truck. One guy is quite banged up, as he gave me a heck of a lot of resistance," I explained. "The rest were cooperative. They are all cuffed, but a couple of them only have flex-cuffs on. You might want to change them to steel wrist cuffs if you have extra. In addition, we would like to give these guys to you as a gift, to take permanently off our hands. As far as I am concerned, they are yours and you can keep them. I don't want them back. Please? Please?" I begged with a smile.

"We understand, and will take them from here. You two can head in and relax a bit; there is fresh coffee and a plate of sandwiches waiting for you," Thom Barker informed us.

Eric and I entered the office and headed straight for the coffee and sandwiches. As I was grabbing for a sandwich, I felt a stab of pain in my hand. It seemed to have swollen more than the last time I looked at it. I wondered if I had broken anything inside. Stewart and I sat down at the large desks that had been shoved together. We ate our sandwiches and sipped the hot coffee, enjoying the relaxed moment in silence and peace, together. Eric Stewart was a damn good man, and proved it today. I staked my life on him as a partner and he did likewise, even though we had met only this morning. He was a great partner through this whole ordeal. I felt he was a friend forever, after today.

I noticed two cassette tape recorders on the desk, and hoped they would eliminate most of the report writing for us. Optimistically, the FBI would get our stories and the facts, and move on from there, with the report responsibilities. That way, Stewart and I would be off the hook until the trial date was set.

I thought I'd bug Stewart, "Ya know, Stewart? With my writing hand not working well, with the swelling, pain and all, you might have to do all the writing and typing, 'cause I am definitely handicapped." I was funning him, to see what he'd say. I knew I was unsuccessful when I heard his reply, "Wonderful! Just my luck," he said with a big, in-your-face grin. "You're not getting off that easily. We will still be doing this together, probably 'til sunrise. Misery loves company, and you're staying with me on this, until the end."

"Does he always have the correct reply?" I thought to myself.

The FBI agents entered the office, with Jim Jensen saying, "What happened to that one guy's face? I hope you can justify it in court, as this looks like brutality." I said, "No, look at my face and shoulder. Like in the movie, 'They drew first blood. I was defending myself.'"

I turned to Eric and said, "You don't have that 'police brutality' problem in Canada, do ya?"

"Right, we will get that all on tape and then on paper with you two signing the document as to what actually happened," Jim said.

My thoughts were about these wildlife thieves. They were guilty until proven innocent, as if they could ever be proven innocent, as long as I was alive.

I still felt angered by that "brutality" comment. "He broke through the flex-cuffs by rubbing them against the steel upright stake on the flatbed truck. Then, set me up to put a saddle blanket over his legs to keep warm, and sucker-smacked me as I laid the blanket down on his legs. Then the fight began," I explained. "Oh, by the way, with this hand swollen from the fight, I don't think I'll be much help writing the reports on this whole situation." I was hoping that any poor, crybaby excuse would relieve me from doing the dreaded paperwork. I hated paperwork.

"This is our case now, gentlemen. You won't have to do any report writing. We will use the tape recorders on the desk to document the story, and then have it typed to a hard copy back at the office," Thom Barker stated, picking up the recorder and turning it on. Agent Barker spoke into the recorder the necessary information: date, time, our names and the incident that would be discussed. Then he said, "Okay, Ernest, explain to us from the beginning what exactly happened, starting yesterday morning."

I began talking. It was all really fresh in my mind because fewer than 48 hours had passed since the first shot. "First, I heard shots in the meadow on my way out, leaving the valley for the season, early yesterday morning." All of a sudden, it seemed like a long time ago, as I explained the events that happened in sequential order. Occasionally, one of the FBI agents would stop me and ask a question for more clarification and description, which made the subject matter more concise and detailed. These guys didn't miss an element, and I was happy to give them everything they needed to know. After an hour and a half, Eric Stewart and I had finished describing all the events, beginning on the previous day, continuing up through our meeting on the morning of the current day, through our combined efforts that day to apprehend the poachers, right up until we turned them over to the FBI. It felt good to have that water under the bridge and be finished with the ordeal.

During the explanation of the poaching incident, Jim Jensen called for an EMT in the area to come down and take a look at my shoulder. The EMT cleaned and redressed the gunshot wound, turned his attention to my throbbing right hand, and said, "I don't think you broke anything, but tomorrow we will get you to the doctor's office where it can be x-rayed."

I thanked him and he left the office and drove home. It was dark outside by then. It was early evening, with stars clearly visible, poking their little lights through the darkened blanket above.

Eric and I got up and walked outside into the chilly, autumn air together. Then we stood beside his truck, to say our goodbyes.

Eric Stewart said, "That's it for us today, Pal, and what a day it has been. I am sure we will be in touch quite a bit over the next few weeks, dealing with this whole fiasco, until the court date is set. I am in my office every morning until ten o'clock. That's the best time to get hold of me." He then stuck his hand out while looking me straight in the eye and said, "Partner, it was one unforgettable day. It was terrific pairing up with you, my friend. Let's plan on getting together sometime soon, have dinner and a few beers and shoot the bull and get to know each other on more regular-guy terms."

"Sounds like a plan. We don't know anything about each other, but our gears meshed together as well as any team. I really don't know what else to say, Eric, except, 'Thanks for all your involvement and help,' I couldn't have done it without you, and still be alive. Thanks pal, I'll be seeing you." We shook hands and I remembered to shake with my left hand that time. Eric climbed into his truck and left for his duty station in Waterton Town, in his home country of

Canada. I stood watching his taillights fade into the darkness, and began feeling very empty and alone.

Agent Barker opened the office door, saw me standing on the sidewalk and yelled, "Russ just radioed in and said the rest of the guys gave themselves up without a fight, and everyone is on their way back here. I thought you would like to know. There were no shooting incidents either."

"Thanks Thom." He stepped back into the warm office. I was alone again in the clear, cold night. I stared up into the frigid, dark, star-filled Big Sky. I was feeling small and insignificant in the universe that my creator had contrived for all of us. I prayed, "Thank you, Lord, for the many blessings I've received. Your safety, guidance and wisdom have kept me alive. I am thankful to still be among the living. You're an awesome God. In your son's name." Amen.

ABOUT THE AUTHOR

Ernie was born in Southern California in the early1950s, and raised in the small town of Sierra Madre. His parents' home was located at the edge of the foothills, where he spent much of his youth exploring and hiking. He began working as a maintenance worker at the Pasadena YMCA's Camp Bluff Lake at the age of 13. He soon became interested in the horses the camp used for trail rides, and eventually became the wrangler, tending to 11 horses and leading trail rides for the campers for most of three summers. Ernie then worked two summers at a Western Riding Ranch Camp in Arizona (Orme Ranch), teaching western saddle equitation. In 1972, he met a gentleman who worked for the Department of the Interior. Through this contact, in 1973 Ernie filled a political appointment position as a backcountry ranger at Polebridge Ranger Station in the North Fork District of Glacier National Park.

Two summers later, he was reassigned to Logging Creek Ranger Station seven miles south of Polebridge Ranger Station. During his second summer, he jacked up the lower Lake Snowshoe Cabin, and replaced the rotten sill logs on that almost-historic structure. A graduate of California State University at Long Beach in Industrial Arts, he landed a job in Columbia Falls, Montana as a wood- and metal-shop teacher. He continued working as a seasonal ranger in summers. His first year as the Belly River Ranger was in 1977. His horsemanship experience once again paid off; as did his wood-working skills that played an important part in the restoration of some of the buildings at Belly River Ranger Station that were from the 1910 era. While building his home, he was injured and was reassigned to Kintla Lake, where he spent three summers as the campground ranger at the 19-site campground. He then requested a reassignment to Cut Bank Ranger Station, on the eastern border of the park spending three summers there, he desired new areas to explore and requested a transfer to Two Medicine Ranger Station. Ernie was married the following winter on Valentine's Day, a month shy of his 35th birthday. Ernie didn't return to the park the next summer because the East Side District Ranger decided, "We need new blood in the park," and proceeded to not rehire some of the long-term, seasonal personnel.

By the time Ernie left the park, he had hiked over 5,000 documented miles, logged on foot and horseback, during his 13 summers of employment for Glacier

Ernie and his wife raised their two sons in the first home he built and retired as a shop teacher for 26 years. He then went on to be a contractor and builder during his retirement years.

Ernie lives in Bigfork, Montana, where he built his last home and is currently semi-retired.